Santa Baby, Bring Me A Dope Boy For Christmas

By

Adrianne

ACKNOWLEDGMENTS

I would like to thank my awesome publishing company, Racquel Williams Presents! We have been rocking together for years, and I'm proud to be an author under a great publishing home.

I appreciate my readers and hope to not disappoint with this novella. I want to dedicate this story to those that I lost this year. May the love that was everlasting in this story resonate the love that I will forever share with each of you. I will forever miss you and love you all: Marian Cunningham, Katherine Cunningham, Brian Lancaster, Frazier D. Grey Jr., Derrick Cunningham, and Krystal Gill-Jones.

SANTA BABY, BRING ME A DOPE BOY FOR CHRISTMAS

-1-

December
Where My Heart Lies

Looking over my life, I had to admit I had experienced more pain than happiness. But, if we never experienced the bad, we would never be able to appreciate that which was good, right? I knew for a fact that my life could've been much worse than it had been, so allow me the moment to introduce myself to you.

My name is December Alise Cruz, and I'm unsure of my father's ethnicity, but my mother is, or was, from the Dominican Republic. If you were wondering why I had any uncertainty, that was because I was left on the doorsteps of St. Francis Children's Home at the age of one! As the story was told to me, there was a note left by my mother (to be opened by myself at age fifteen) and my birth certificate.

No need for all the sympathy for me because the sisters of St. Francis were the best mothers and nurturers that us kids could ever ask for! I would forever wonder about my mother and her

SANTA BABY, BRING ME A DOPE BOY FOR CHRISTMAS

circumstances, but I knew I was loved and cared for at the orphanage. I had always been a shy and more reserved child. Most kids at the home were attention seekers, especially on 'Visitor's Day.' The orphanage had those once a month wherein selective couples would visit and spend the day with all of us kids. If we were well-liked, we could be prospects for adoption. But that was never something that I wanted. I loved the sisters, and St. Francis was my home. Sister Sophie, my absolute favorite, always knew to look for me hidden under her wooden desk in her office. She knew me so well that she often left the office door cracked for easy access for me.

She would always knock on the top of the desk after the couples were gone and tell me that it was safe to show my beautiful face again. Sister Sophie and myself had the closest bond, but they were all gems in my eyes. I could never imagine my life without them because they were all that I knew. I used to dream about my mom or both parents reappearing with gifts and hugs to reclaim me, but that was never the case. I also didn't like the feel of being 'moving cattle' that was examined by couples for purchase if you caught my metaphor. Some of those couples gave me the creeps, and I couldn't imagine their real intentions from what I saw. I mean, what if they locked kids in the basement for fun? Or starved them or only let them out to work their land or some craziness like that? Once we left the orphanage, it was not like we could call and return, so I didn't want to risk the chance of being with a terrible family.

I never had any real friends like the rest of the kids that lived there. I had mentioned my shyness in the beginning. I always felt like I didn't quite fit in with the rest of the Black kids because my looks were not equal to theirs. I had the mocha complexion, but due to my Dominican roots, I had wavy-curly, black hair and hazel eyes. My small and delicate frame often made me a target for the house bullies, such as Shameka. We were roomed according to our age groups. There were rooms for the newborns to age three, then ages four to six, seven to ten, eleven to thirteen, and the other teens had bigger dorm quarters. Boys and girls were separated after age six.

We had all our classes in the adjoined building next to the orphanage, Monday through Friday, just like regular school kids. But the sisters always incorporated religion into our daily regimen. There was a lavish chapel and chorus group that rehearsed on Saturdays before and after mass.

SANTA BABY, BRING ME A DOPE BOY FOR CHRISTMAS

By age seven, I had moved into the dorm rooms with other girls my age, and of course, Shameka was on my case. She hated the fact that my hair was a better grade than hers and several other Black girls. She would tug on my two long ponytails or call me names like 'half-breed' or things like that. I was never a real fighter and would usually cry from her torture or run to Sister Sophie. The other girls would cheer her on because of fear that she would turn on them. So, most times, I would eat lunch alone or skip it all together to avoid her ass. After experiencing a typical morning of Shameka's rants and torment, I cried in one of the bathrooms, ran some water on my face, and prayed that God would send me someone to protect me from her bullying ways. I said that prayer so often that I knew God was tired of it, but I held my faith and prayed that God would intervene sooner than later.

On that day, we were just beginning math class, one of my favorite subjects. Sister Edith was doing her roll call for the class when there was a knock on the door.

"Settle down, class." Sister Edith tapped her ruler on her wooden desk. She was a short and chunky lady. Shameka always joked that she waddled when she walked, like a duck. There were still a few whispers around the class, but everyone calmed down. Sister Edith walked over to the classroom door and stepped into the hallway.

"Half-breed, half-breed." Shemeka teased me from the back of the room. "She's scared because the sister stepped out of the room!" She laughed and threw wadded up paper at the back of my head. I felt the tears form in my eyes, but suddenly, the sister emerged once more but with an unfamiliar face by her side.

"Class," Sister Edith cleared her throat, and we were all at full attention, "I want you all to welcome a new student and child to our extended family. This is D'Angelo, and I want you all to be courteous and show the likeness of Jesus! This means you too, Shameka Denise!"

"Why you had to call me out like that, Sister Edith?" Shameka whined and portrayed a ray of innocence. "I don't have any problems with my friends in here, just the ones that think they better than the rest of us!"

"And what is that supposed to mean?" Sister Edith raised her brow at Shemeka, but everyone knew that was directed towards me.

"Nothing, Sister." Shameka sighed. "I volunteer to be D'Angelo's buddy for the week and show him the ins and outs if you need me to."

I heard a few of Shameka's flock mention his cuteness, and I was sure that was why she volunteered in the first place. I shyly glanced at the new kid. He was quite tall for the age of eight but had the most magnetic presence and hazel eyes that matched mine. His complexion was that of coffee with extra cream, and his deep dimples made me blush.

"I do appreciate your gesture, Shameka." Sister Edith smiled. "But I think I will let December buddy up with him."

"December!" Shameka shrieked. "Ughh, but why her?"

"Yeah." I twisted my face. "Why me?"

"Shut up, hater!" Shameka ranted. "I volunteered, Sister. Plus, December doesn't even talk to people. Until just now, I was beginning to think the cat stole her tongue or something!"

"Well," Sister Edith replied with a smile. "Being D'Angelo's buddy will give her the opportunity to make a new friend and break out of her shy shell. Okay? So, it's settled. D'Angelo, have a seat next to December, and the rest of you, let's get ready for our math lesson."

I felt a flutter of butterflies arise in my gut as I glanced over at the new kid. He simply gave me a smile and comforting head nod. I felt my face flush from his attention, but maybe he was the friend that God had placed in my path. I knew one thing was for certain. Shemeka was madder than hell about it, so I would have to watch my back more than ever.

I nervously showed D'Angelo the lays of the land and where his dorm and supplies were kept here. He didn't say much to me at first, but by lunchtime, he finally decided to spark up a conversation with me.

"So," he began. "What's with you and the Black gorilla over there?"

"What?" I giggled slightly and noticed he was pointing at Shameka.

"I can't remember her name." He laughed at his own joke. "So, I just called her what she reminds me of."

"That's Shemeka," I replied in a whisper with shifty eyes.

"Yeah, so what's her issue with you?" He probed further.

"She's never really liked me. I guess I'm just really quiet and not loud or as popular as the rest of her crowd."

"You're pretty, and she just hates you for it." He nudged my shoulder, and I felt an electric shock from his touch. My face turned a shade of red which was hard for a kid with such a mocha color.

"You-you think I'm pretty?" I glanced at his welcoming face and shyly looked away.

"Duh." He teased and stuck his tongue out at me. "She thinks so too. That's why she gives you such a hard time! I mean, just look at her. She looks like a skid mark with a brillo pad on her head for hair!"

We both burst out laughin', and that drew attention from many of the kids in the lunchroom. I couldn't remember ever laughing that hard in my short life. It felt so good, and I started to relax and speak frequently to my new buddy. Over the next few weeks, D'Angelo told me about what landed him in the orphanage. His parents were both junkies and were unable to care for him. He took care of himself and learned to fight or steal to survive. After his father overdosed a few months prior, his mom disappeared and left him in an abandoned house. He had stopped going to school, and one of his teachers spotted him on a street corner, trying to make a few sales. Did I mention that D'Angelo was only eight years old when he came to the orphanage? That was very young to be a dope dealer, but I guess he had to do what he had to in order to survive. He said he was placed with a few family members. but his rage and street ways were too much for them to handle. So, he ended up at St. Francis with the rest of us. I hated his life circumstances but was grateful that he was with me, and we soon became best friends.

***

D'Angelo had helped me come out of my shell over the next few years. By age twelve, I had more friends than enemies, but Shemeka always seemed to try me whenever she had the opportunity. She was still the ugly gorilla that D'Angelo called her years ago, but some of the boys seemed to like her because she grew breasts and put out with the older boys. I was still petite with a bird chest, but I did have a little something poking from the back.

The wintertime was approaching, and the sisters always went all out for the birth of Jesus in extravagant fashion. I loved the holiday season because my birthday was the 31st of December. I may have not had the traditional family dynamics, but I had the sisters and D'Angelo to love me. I was blessed and thankful for that.

"Okay, children." Sister Sophie clapped her hands in the theater room to grab our attention. "As you know, 'tis the season once again! And we will be looking for volunteers this year for the Nativity scenes and birth of our savior, Jesus Christ! I will have a sign-up sheet available on my desk. We will also need help with props and costumes for the actors."

"I would love to play the role of Mary, Sister Sophie." Shameka raised her hand and fluttered her eyes rapidly.

"That's fine with me, Shameka." Sister Sophie nodded and jotted something down on her notepad.

"I would love for D'Angelo to be my Joseph," Shameka continued. "And maybe his lil' flunky, December, could be our baby Jesus!"

I heard a few cackles from her flock in the back of the room, but I tried to pay them no attention. D'Angelo read my face and immediately raised his hand in the class.

"Yes, D'Angelo," Sister Sophie responded.

"Umm." He stood and walked to the front of the class. "As much as I would like to participate in the play this year, I will have to decline Shameka's offer to play her Joseph."

"Why is that?" Shameka frowned and squinted her bucked eyes.

"Because Mary was a virgin, which you haven't been for some time now. Not to mention, I'on wanna stand next to a damn gorilla! Someone needs to take yo' ass back to the zoo where you belong!" D'Angelo pointed and laughed.

"LANGUAGE!" Sister Sophie scolded, but I could tell she wanted to laugh behind that stern glance.

Shameka was so shocked from his remarks and the laughter from the rest of the kids that she exited the theater room and was followed by a few of her friends. Sister Sophie advised the rest of us to settle down, and D'Angelo was sent to detention for the rest of that week. He simply shrugged his shoulders and gave me a wink. I knew he only sacrificed his free time for me, and that meant the world to me.

"I can't believe you clowned Shemeka like that." I snickered as we made our way to the rec room.

"It needed to be said," D'Angelo joked and received a few high fives from other kids in our age group. "She needs to know her place with me. I could never be interested in her trashy ass, and now she knows not to come for me or my bestie."

"I'm used to her coming for me." I shrugged my shoulders and sighed.

"That's the point, DeeDee." D'Angelo frowned at me. He gave me the nickname DeeDee, and I called him Gelo. "Aren't you tired of that shit? I mean, c'mon, girl. You know I got your back, but sooner or later, you gotta put that girl in her place. I won't always be around, and the sooner you check her, the sooner she will leave you alone!"

"Who gon check me?" Shemeka gave me a slight shove and tapped her chest victoriously.

"Girl, bye!" D'Angelo fanned her away. "I already did that, or did you forget?"

"I let you get away with it because you're sexy as hell," she admitted. "But that lil' bitch you hang with, now she knows better."

"Ain't nobody scared of you," D'Angelo continued, and a crowd started to form around us.

"You might not be," Shameka replied. "But you can't speak for the half-breed!"

I had grown tired of Shameka and her shit. D'Angelo looked over at me, and his facial expressions told me to say something or react in any way. I closed my eyes, took a few deep breathes, and dropped my reading book on the ground. I balled up my fists and charged my nemesis head on!

"I'M SICK OF YOUR SHIT, SHEMEKA!" I punched her dead in the face and watched her fall to the ground while other kids cheered me on. "IT'S NOT MY FAULT THAT I HAVE GOOD HAIR AND DON'T LOOK LIKE A BEAST INSTEAD OF A BEAUTY! KEEP MY DAMN NAME OUTTA YO MOUTH, YOU STANK SLUT!"

I punched and kicked her with a newfound independence I had never known. She got a few licks on me, but I stayed mounted on top of her until two of the sisters pried me off her kickin' and screamin'!

"THIS AIN'T OVER!" Shameka was dragged away in the opposite direction from me, but I did get the best of her.

"I'M NOT AFRAID OF YOU! SO, IF IT'S ON, THEN IT'S ON!" I spat out, and D'Angelo was still by my side.

SANTA BABY, BRING ME A DOPE BOY FOR CHRISTMAS

"You heard what she said," D'Angelo teased. "Time to lock that gorilla back in her cage! Bye-bye now!"

I was later given two weeks of detention, and the sisters made Shameka and I apologize to one another for our altercation. It was far from heartfelt, but at least I had finally stood up for myself, and it felt amazing. My bestie made me feel untouchable, and at that moment, I knew that I loved him. I only wondered how deep his feelings went for me. Did he only see me as a friend, or was there a possibility for something more in the future? I was still too shy to say anything about that, but for the first time in my life, I thought I had found a home for my heart in D'Angelo Carter.

-2-

December
When Seasons Change

By the time I reached fourteen, Shameka and I had engaged in several more fights, but I was always victorious. I was no longer the shy girl that ducked or dodged her insults like before. Whether D'Angelo was present or not, I grew to handle my own, and I only hoped that Shameka would take the hint and chill out. I loved the new living quarters that I shared with three other girls in my age group. As I stated before, the older teens received more space and accessibility in the orphanage. There were four to a room, and some of the teens were able to work part-time jobs, depending on their good behavior and supervision from the sisters. There were less kids between the ages of fourteen to eighteen, mostly because we were either adopted before that age, and it was harder to place us. But I was happy with my living situation, and not to mention, my bestie was across the hall in his dorm with the guys.

D'Angelo excelled in most sports and was smart, even though he rarely paid attention in many of our classes. He was more interested in girls and longed for the street life and fast money. I guess you could take the boy out of the hood, but you couldn't take the hood out of him! It didn't make things any better that the orphanage was smack dab in the hood. Yes, we had a gated area, but most of the teens found ways to sneak out, and D'Angelo was no exception to that rule. Him and a couple of the guys would pretend to work jobs but were really interested in the street life and fattening their pockets.

"So, what are your plans for when you get outta here?" Destiny, one of my roommates, asked while we relaxed in our room. "I can't wait to turn eighteen and get my own place. Maybe look for one of my older siblings or leave Alabama all together."

"I heard that." Tabitha, another teen, snickered. "It doesn't seem like any of the couples are interested in adopting a kid that's fifteen or older. So, I'm just tryin' to stack my money from the Piggly Wiggly and save for a place."

"Sounds like a plan to me." Destiny rejoiced while she continued to braid Tabitha's hair in a few cornrows. "I thought about going to beauty school, but I don't know."

"I think that would be the move for you." I applauded her dreams. "There's not too much you can't do to our heads, and I appreciate it. If it was up to me, I would just wear my hair in a ponytail for the rest of my life!"

"Thanks, boo." Destiny beamed with delight. "But I love styling your hair. You lucked up with that good shit. And you look like a model when you wear it straight or with flowing curls."

I immediately blushed and gave myself a look over in the mirror that hung on our wall. I now stood five foot five, grew some B-cup titties, and had a tight waist with curves to match. My flawless mocha complexion was complimented with my slanted hazel eyes. I ran my hands through my straightened hair and watched it fall to the middle of my back.

"Thanks, boo." I gave her a wink and applied a little lip gloss to my pouty lips. "I often wonder how I would look with a shorter hairstyle."

"Ughh." Tabitha rolled her eyes playfully.

"Why do the chicks with good hair always wanna cut their shit? Here I am, adding hair to my shit, andyou don't want yours!"

"It was just a thought." I shrugged my shoulders and glanced out the hallway as I heard my bestie's voice vibrate from his dorm.

SANTA BABY, BRING ME A DOPE BOY FOR CHRISTMAS

"You must be lookin' for you boo thang." Destiny teased. "Don't worry. I'm sure he will be over here in a few to check on you."

"Stop all of that." I fanned her away but felt myself blush from embarrassment. There was no denying the way that I felt for D'Angelo, and others caught on to it. But he was quite the heartbreaker, so I kept my true feelings on the inside as much as possible. "Me and Gelo are just friends, and you know that!"

"I hear ya, boo," Destiny continued. "But even a blind man can see that you would want more than that. I know you didn't ask for my opinion."

"I never do." I fired back sarcastically.

"But I'ma speak my peace." She smiled while she finished one of Tabitha's braids. "I think you should shoot your shot with him. I mean, you are the best of friends, but there could be more to it. Everyone knows how the two of you feel about each other, girl! So, why hide it from yourselves?"

"That's my bestie." I became defensive. "But we all know that he's a little on the hoeish side! I'on wanna compete with all of that."

"You trippin'." Tabitha joked. "I think if he knew your true feelings, he'd drop all of them ducks for you!"

"Facts!" Destiny chimed in.

"Yeah, okay!" I nodded nervously and tried to change the subject with my roommates. But there was a part of me that was curious about their suggestion. Of course, I wanted to date D'Angelo, but I was fearful of his rejection. And I would never want to jeopardize the friendship that we shared.

"What are you Gals in here cacklin' about?" D'Angelo tapped on our bedroom door and peeked his head inside the room.

"Wouldn't you like to know." Destiny smiled and glanced over at me.

I couldn't deny the look of desire that graced my face whenever D'Angelo entered a room. At age fifteen, he stood a whooping five foot ten inches. He had a muscular build, and his caramel skin and hazel eyes were the talk of the teenage girls! He always rocked dreads, and Destiny kept them looking flawless every two weeks. He was everything that I wanted but desired by the rest of these girls as well. That always bothered me. I hated to feel so jealous, but my heart couldn't help it.

"Anyways." D'Angelo fanned them off and plopped down on my bed with me. "What's good with you, bestie? You ready to hang or nawl?"

"We can." I nodded and bid farewell to my girls. "I'll meet you down the hall. I gotta look for that book I was reading. I need to return it to the library."

"Aite then." He winked and exited the room while I grabbed the book from my book bag.

"Don't forget what we discussed earlier, girl," Destiny jabbed. "Let him know how you feel. You got his heart, so shoot your shot, boo!"

"I will see y'all later!" I threw up the peace sign and walked down the hallway to my bestie.

Just as I had stated earlier, D'Angelo owned a room, and the chicken heads were all over him. While I walked towards him, I tried to keep my composure while his newest boo was hanging on his hip with her chicks beside her. Now, I never had any beef with Ciarra, but the fact that I knew she was smashin' the guy I loved didn't set too well with me.

"Hey, bestie." D'Angelo smiled while he hugged his lil' girlfriend. "I wondered what was takin' you so long."

"Seems to me that you was doin' just fine before I got here." I glanced at the flock of chicks surrounding him.

"Aww, she's a lil' jelly!" Ciarra teased. "I just missed my boo. I guess you would understand if you ever decided to venture out and get a boo of your own!"

"The shade." Her friend, Camille, cackled.

"But on some real, I heard that boy, Daniel, was feelin' you, girl. He's been peepin' you for a minute.I could hook y'all up if you wanted me to."

"Hook her up with that weak ass nigga, Daniel?" D'Angelo's face immediately frowned up. "Over my dead body! DeeDee don't need none of y'all hookin' her up with anybody! She's good just the way she is, ya heard?"

"Why you always cock blockin' her?" Ciarra snapped back. "Maybe if she had a dude of her own, we would be able to spend more time together!"

"Girl, bye!" D'Angelo fired back. "We spend plenty time together. Didn't I just see yo' ass this morning and last night? Fuck you mean? Don't try that shit with me."

"Hello," I interjected. "I am standing right here! I appreciate the gesture, Camille. You can tell Daniel to come step to me when you see him."

SANTA BABY, BRING ME A DOPE BOY FOR CHRISTMAS

"The fuck?" D'Angelo roared and grabbed me by the arm to storm off.

"Will do, boo!" Camille shouted as we walked away from them.

I attempted to jerk my arm away from my bestie, but he held a tight grip on me and didn't say a word until we made it to the library.

"What's wrong with you, Gelo?" I searched his face.

"You know damn well what's wrong," he replied through clenched teeth. "Why would you even consider Daniel's clown ass? I have beat his ass more than once, and plus, he's soft as Charmin tissue! Is that the type of dude that you want to be with?"

"It's not that serious, is it?" I replied with a shrug. "I mean, you always have a chick on your arm. And you never see me clownin' about your girlfriend choices! So, why can't I find a guy to occupy my time? I wouldn't mind having a boyfriend or someone to spend time with."

"I'm not goin' there with you, DeeDee!" He continued to frown as we made our way to return my library book. "You gon get lil' buddy fucked up!

Plus, you got me to spend time with! Just focus on school and becoming the nurse that you wanna be. None of these fools are right for you in here! You're above all of that shit!"

"That's a little hypocritical, don't you think?" I rolled my eyes at him, and we made our way to the rec room.

"What's that supposed to mean?" He gave an innocent look, and I felt my heart flutter once more.

"You date any and everyone you want to in here." I poked him in his chest with my other hand on my hip. "But you wanna throw shade when a guy shows interest in me! Who are you saving me for? I mean, really!"

"Just drop it, okay?" He frowned and glanced away from my trance. I could tell that there was a mystery hidden in his eyes, but he refused to confess it to me.

"Nawl, I don't think so!" I rebelled against him. "If it's okay for you to fuck and date whoever, there shouldn't be a problem with me talkin' to Daniel or anyone else up in here! We are best friends, but you are not my daddy or my man!"

"I said what I said, DeeDee!" He gave me a stern look and grabbed my delicate hand inside of his own. "You deserve better than the fools in here. And yeah, I fuck with these chicken heads, but that has nothing to do with you! You know that I put you in a higher caliber than theses hoes! So, don't get Daniel or the rest of these clowns knocked off because you in yo' feelings!"

"Whatever, Gelo." I rolled my eyes at him, but he immediately put a smile on my face by picking me up and spinning me around. He wasn't the best at expressin' his feelings, but he couldn't stand me being upset with him.

"Stop bein' like that with me." He pouted and melted my heart once more. "Plus, I had something I wanted to talk to you about."

"And what's that?" I questioned as we sat on the bleachers and watched a few of the guys playin' basketball.

"Your birthday is coming up soon." He smiled and playfully jabbed me in my ribs.

"Yeah, and?" I tried to play off my excitement behind it.

"Don't even try to act like that with me." He commenced to tickle my sides, and I caved in. "I know this is a symbolic year for you. Are you nervous about that note your mom left you?"

"Yeah, I'm nervous." I took a few deep breaths. "Thanks for bringing it back up, bestie! I just don't understand why I needed to read it at age fifteen instead of before that. I mean, what difference did that make? It's not like my mom is here to save me! She dropped me off almost fourteen years ago, and I haven't heard from her since then."

"I know that's a hurtful feeling." D'Angelo's face softened. "All of us kids know what it's like to feel abandoned. That's why most of us are in here. But you know you got me for life. And I will be right there with you to read it if that's what you want."

"You already know I want you there." I pushed him playfully.

"Well, you know you got me." He winked at me.

"Are you this good of a boyfriend to all of them chicks you got?" I teased.

"What do you mean?" He raised his eyebrow slightly.

"I mean the caring way that you are with me." I pointed out. "Are you like that with Ciarra or the rest of them girls?"

"Now," he breathed heavily, "you know that I treat them hoes accordingly. And don't ever compare yourself to any of them. They know their roles, and that's what it is!"

"Seems like to me," I paused before I finished my sentence, "if you treat me better than them, I should be the one you with and not the rest of them girls. But it's cool. I don't wanna ruin your player persona, playboy!"

"You always got the jokes." He smiled nervously and commenced to tickle me.

I may have had the jokes for him, but there was a part of me that was dead ass serious. I wasn't sure if he paid any attention to it, so I decided to drop the subject and speak on other things. I did have my birthday approaching, and I was worried about the note my mom had left for me. Would she divulge her whereabouts or at least let me know why she abandoned me? I guess I would have to wait another week to find out her truth.

-3-

December
There's No Goin' Back Now

It was finally my birthday, and I was a basketful of nerves and anxiety. My roommates spared no expense on pampering me with cosmetics and a few trinkets for my special day. I tried to show my appreciation to them, but my thought reverted to that note that my mom left for me. I thought about not reading it and just throwing it away! I didn't want to ruin my day with tears and unanswered or unresolved feelings. Even if I read the note, I wouldn't be able to get the real resolutions from my mother, so why bother?

"There's a birthday girl in the building!" D'Angelo knocked on our bedroom door in his usual corky manner.

"Yes, and she's looking fabulous. Don't you think?" Destiny gave herself a pat on the back. She had taught me the basics when it came to applying foundation and a bit of mascara, eye liner, and lipstick for more highlights. I wore a fitted Alabama football jersey, and some fitted jeans that hugged my curves perfectly. I managed to afford some new red and grey J's that fit my outfit perfectly. I had saved a few weeks from my job at the local grocery store.

They usually didn't hire teens my age, but the sisters put in a good word for me, and the money was appreciated.

"Yeah." D'Angelo appeared choked up with his words as he gave me a detailed look over. "She's definitely lookin' nice."

"Now, all she needs is a boo or a date for the night," Tabitha jabbed.

"I'on know about all of that shit." D'Angelo fumed and gave me a hug.

"Always the hater I see." I joked with him.

"But thanks for the compliment. I guess."

"Don't forget what I told you the other day." He almost whispered. I knew he was referring to the convo about me being better than the rest of the chicken heads or whatever.

"Yeah, yeah." I punched him playfully.

"But you really look nice, girl." Destiny smiled with her accomplishments. "Did you ever talk with Daniel, or has that ship sailed?"

"Fuck you mean?" D'Angelo blurted out. "That ship never made it to the dock! Let's get outta here, DeeDee!"

"The king has spoken." Tabitha chuckled with Destiny.

"See you guys a little later." I rolled my eyes and followed my bestie out of the dorm room.

"I can't believe you're still actin' like that, Gelo! I thought we discussed this already."

"I said what I said, girl!" he continued. "But enough about that clown! What did you wanna do today? I got some extra bread, so it's whatever you like today!"

We saw Sister Sophie poke her head out of her office door while we stood in the hallway.

"December, can you come in here please?" She waved with a smile.

"I guess it's about that time." My bestie sighed and grabbed my hand for support.

Although I felt the tears form in my eyes, I refused to let them fall. I had my support system with me, so whatever was on that note would not get the best of me. Well, at least that was what I told myself.

"Yes, ma'am," I replied as D'Angelo closed the door behind us. We both took seats on the opposite side of Sister Sophie's desk while she rummaged through her file cabinet.

"I want to begin by saying happy birthday to you, December." She walked from behind her desk and gave me a big hug and kiss on my forehead. "I know you have been anxious about this birthday. But you know that God is always in control, and you are loved right here! We are all here for you. If you would like for me to step out while you read the note, that's fine with me."

"She knows I'm not goin' anywhere." D'Angelo held onto my hand while he spoke his peace.

"I already knew that to be true." Sister Sophie smiled at the both of us. "You have always been the best friend to December. With that being said, I will leave the two of you in here. I will be in the chapel if you need me, December."

"Thanks so much, Sister Sophie." I gave her a slight smile and watched as she exited the office. "Ugh, I don't know if I can do this, Gelo! I don't wanna know what it says! I don't want my day to be ruined with this crap!"

"I can truly understand." D'Angelo wrapped his strong arms around me for comfort. "But you know I'm right here with you. We can read it together if that makes you feel better."

I simply gave him a head nod as I opened the manilla envelope and prepared myself for the words of my mother.

'Dearest December,

I was only fourteen years old when I was raped and pregnant with you! The son of the family that sponsored me to the states was my inflictor! He knew that my English wasn't that good at the time, and no one would believe me if I was to tell on him. He was seventeen at the time, and his mother put his ass on a pedestal... So, I hid my pregnancy and paternity for as long as I could because I was in a foreign land and didn't want to risk your health or well-being. But as time went on, I began to show, and the school I attended alerted my sponsor family of my situation.

I was hounded constantly and eventually told them the truth. Of course, the boy denied it and made it seem like I came on to him. I was only a kid! I didn't know anything about sex or boys! I felt so much shame but knew that I wouldn't be welcomed back home to the Dominican Republic. So, what did I do? I gave birth to you and was put out on the streets after the hospital released me! So, I was a fifteen-year-old immigrant with nowhere to go and a baby to take care of! I tried my best, but I didn't have money for a sitter and jobs wouldn't hire me because of my age and lack of education.

SANTA BABY, BRING ME A DOPE BOY FOR CHRISTMAS

I sold my body. What other options did I have? It allowed me to feed you, and I found refuge in a few abandoned houses. But over that year, I found a few of the tricks tryin' to touch you, and they would ask questions about you in a reckless way. I didn't want any harm to come your way because of the mistakes I made. So, one day while I was walking with you in my arms, I strolled past St. Francis Children's Home. I saw a few nuns outside tending a garden, and they seemed so nice and genuine. They even offered me a meal and a place to wash up. I thought long and hard about it and decided it was the best place for you.

Don't ever think that I didn't love you because that's not the case at all. I loved you more than anything, and I wanted you to be safe and have a better life than I could offer to you. I hope that one day you will find it in your heart to forgive me for leaving you. But know that I didn't have the means to care for you. I will try to survive on my own, but I want your life to be successful. My relationship with my family has been strained since I arrived in the states, but I do have an older sister, Camille Cruz. She's several years older than me. I did try to reach out to her while I was on the streets, but due to the family strain, she never called back. Enclosed is the last known number I had for her and an estimated address. Maybe she will show more mercy on you because you're her innocent niece. Happy 15th birthday, baby girl. Know that I will always love you. And if you're wondering why I wanted you to read this letter at age 15… it's because it's the age I was when I had to give you up. So, just imagine being 15 with a baby to care for and nowhere to go.

Love always,
Sophia Cruz'

I read those words and was inconsolable. My heart ached for my young mother, and I couldn't begin to imagine the state of mind that she went through given her situation. I had spent all these years resenting her for leaving but never knew she was raped and homeless with me. The more I cried, the more I felt that hatred in my heart being released. The letter was wet from my tears, and when I glanced at D'Angelo, I saw his eyes were equally as moist. We sat in the sister's office for what seemed to be an eternity and just held one another. There was no need for words to be spoken. We just fed off one another's energy.

"That was so damn heavy." D'Angelo finally broke the silence between us and gently kissed me on the forehead. "I wish I had some words to make the pain go away, but I'm at a real loss here, best friend."

"You can say that again." I signed and grabbed a few tissues from the desk to blow my nose. "I just really appreciate your being here with me. I don't think I would be able to be this strong without you. Thanks so much, Gelo! I love you for being the friend that I needed."

I gave him a shy first kiss and regretted it at first. I caught him off guard, but instead of pushing me away, he embraced my face with the palm of his hands and drew me in closer for a longer kiss. I felt my body melt, and my kitty tingled from his touch. I wondered if that was his way of saying he loved me just as much. For the moment, I decided to just go with it.

"I think we should get out of here." He breathed and looked through my soul with compassion. "I'd hate for the sister to come back and punish us for that kiss."

"I guess it was a mistake." I shyly looked away from him and stood to my feet.

He immediately grabbed me by the hand, placed the note back in the envelope, and pulled me closer to him.

"Come with me," he stated, and we made our way to his dorm room. After we entered the room, he closed the door behind us and grabbed his phone from his back pocket. He dialed a number and conversed a few minutes with someone on the other end.

"...yeah, can you do that for me?" D'Angelo referred to whoever was on the phone.

"Okay, I appreciate it, bro. You know I got you!"

He hung up the phone, sat on his bed, and signaled for me to join him.

"Stop actin' scary and come sit beside me, December."

"December?" I replied jokingly. "What happened to DeeDee?"

"I'on know." He shrugged his shoulders and leaned in for another kiss. "She's always my bestie. But right now, I'm interested in this young lady named December. I think that I been sleepin' on her for long enough. What do you think about that?"

"What are you trying to say?" I tried to contain my composure, but in my heart, I had waited years for this moment.

"I can't keep denying the way I feel about you." He sighed. "And don't worry about someone walkin' in on us. I got my homies watching the hallway for us. So, kick back and just relax."

"Deny your feelings?" I probed further as he planted kisses all over my face and neck.

"Can we revisit that convo?"

"I don't want you talkin' to none of these fools in here because I want you for myself." He finally admitted. "Can't you tell all of that? Did I really have to say it?"

"Was it that hard for you to say?" I raised a brow at him while I scooted back on his bed.

"I can show you better than I can tell you."

He continued to plant kisses all over my face and neck, and I felt his hands roaming over my perky breasts. These feelings and actions were all new to me, and I was sure he could feel my body tremble from his touch.

"Relax, girl." He chuckled while he climbed on top of me. "You know I got you, right?"

I simply nodded and allowed him to stick his tongue down my throat while he separated my legs and laid between them.

"Let me grab a few things." He slid off the bed slowly. "I'll be right back."

He stood to his feet and removed his t-shirt and sweatpants. He then went into the bathroom, grabbed a bath towel, and placed it on the bed. He also went over to his dresser and grabbed a condom before returning to the bed with me.

"Wow, I can't believe this is actually happening." I breathed with anticipation.

"We don't have to do anything that you don't feel ready to do."

"I understand all of that." I bit my bottom lip.

"But I am in love with you, Gelo. I have felt like this for so long, but I thought you only viewed me as a friend. There's honestly no one else that I would want to share this experience with but you."

"That's what I was waiting to hear, girl." He climbed on top of me, and I helped remove all my clothes except for my bra and panties. I was self-conscious about my body as he stared back at me. "You are absolutely beautiful. Ain't no way in hell I could ever be okay with another dude touchin' on you. You belong to me!"

"Forever." I sighed and wiggled out of my panties and bra.

"And for always."

-4-

December
Pullin' Heart Strings

To say that I was on cloud nine after D'Angelo and I did the do would be an understatement. We confessed our love for one another. From that day forward, he cancelled all his hoes, and I was the only one for him. We held hands, stole intimate kisses, and had sex like rabbits for the next few months. D'Angelo seemed to have our future planned out for the both of us. He was confident that he would be that nigga (dope boy) on the streets, and then, he could give me the life that he felt I deserved. But I was still content with going to college and becoming a nurse to help others.

D'Angelo wasn't against my dreams, but I hated the fact that he didn't have a better game plan for his own dreams. The life of a dope boy was so risky, but he said he couldn't see himself punchin' a time clock or answering to another man for money. I tried my best to talk him out of it, but that shit went in one ear and out of the other one.

For the meantime, I was happy having the love of my life by my side. I only hoped that he would change the way he thought over time. I had also asked the sisters to look for my aunt, Camille. Since I knew I had family somewhere, I wanted the opportunity to meet with her. I wondered if she ever contacted my mother or why there was a family beef between them.

"What are you over there thinkin' about, beautiful?" D'Angelo stole a few kisses while I stared off into space in the lunchroom.

"Ughh." Destiny teased us. "Get a damn room you two."

"Don't you worry about that," D'Angelo laughed. "We got a few of those on deck."

"Just nasty." Tabitha chuckled, and my girls excused themselves from the table.

"Hey, boo." I planted another kiss on his lips before he sat beside me. "I was just thinkin' about the future and things of that nature."

"Is that right?" He winked and gave me a hug. "I guess that's cool as long as I'm included in it."

"Now, you already know." I rolled my eyes at him playfully.

"Forever?" he asked.

"And always." I finished our motto.

"Real spit!" He chuckled and stole a few fries from my lunch tray.

"So, what did you wanna do for your birthday?" I asked. D'Angelo would be turning sixteen on February 12th.

"I hadn't given it much thought for real." He scratched his temple sneakily. "I already got everything I want!"

"Good answer." I winked at him. "But seriously, we gotta do something special for your birthday. I got some money saved up, so it's whatever you like, boo!"

"You know your money is no good with me, girl!" He placed his fingers across my lips. "Don't even play yourself like that! I guess we can grab a bite to eat or somethin' like that."

"Okay, sounds good to me," I replied and noticed he was focused on the phone more than our conversation. "Do you need to handle that because it seems to have more of your attention than I do?"

"Don't be like that, boo." He smiled and held me close to him. "Just handlin' some biz with my boys. You know how that goes."

Yeah, I knew what he meant. D'Angelo had planned on being jumped into the gang, Stanton Ave Boyz. I was against it, but of course, he didn't wanna hear any of that. He had been skippin' classes and spendin' more of his time in the hood and makin' sales for them Boyz. Every time he left the orphanage, my heart skipped a beat. I was fearful that harm could come his way, and I couldn't imagine life without him.

"…Hell yeah." D'Angelo smiled from his phone convo. "Thanks, bro… Yeah, that's whassup!"

"What was all of that about?" I questioned with concern.

"There you go," he teased. "Always wanting to know everything! Can yo' man surprise you sometimes?"

"I guess so." I shrugged my shoulders.

"It has something that I wanted to do for my birthday." He hinted to me. "Do you still have to work this weekend?"

"Yeah," I answered. "But I let them know I may need the weekend off, so if your surprise is around my work hours, let me know, so I can plan accordingly."

"I love the way you think, babe." He smiled and showed those sexy dimples. "I think you should call out for Saturday because we got plans."

"That's not a problem." I smiled. "So, are you gonna walk me to work in a little bit?"

"Don't I always?" He frowned slightly, but I loved to tease him.

D'Angelo's birthday weekend was in full swing, and I made sure to give him an extra dose of this loving because of it. I made sure to call out from work, so I waited for him to come to my room for our date and surprise that he had planned for the evening.

"Yo boo turned sixteen, huh?" Destiny styled my hair in flowing curls, and I had painted my nails and applied a little lip gloss to my pouty lips.

"Yeah." I smiled instantaneously. "I know we are going to eat, but he's got something else up his sleeve too."

"I'm sure you're gonna love it." Destiny beamed.

"Why do I have the feeling that you know more than what you're tellin' me?"

"Why would you assume that?" She smiled as she sprayed some oil sheen over my hair.

"You look amazing. Now, go ahead and get dressed and get outta here!"

There was some fuckery going on, but I guessed I would have to stay in the dark for the time being. I went ahead and got dressed, but I was skeptical because I hated being in the dark with D'Angelo and his surprises.

"There's my beautiful baby." D'Angelo tapped on my bedroom door and admired me before ravishing me with kisses. "You makin' me wanna change dinner plans. You lookin' like a full course meal!"

"Boy, stop!" I laughed while I blushed uncontrollably.

We made our way to the Italian restaurant three blocks down from the orphanage. It was a known hangout for the older kids, and they served the best homemade pizzas in the city. I still managed to surprise my boo with a customized gold charm with the 14-carat necklace to match. I thought long and hard about a symbol that best depicted my love for D'Angelo. I thought the infinity sign summed it up. So, I ordered a golden infinity symbol with our initials engraved on the opposite side of it. I could tell my gift touched his heart, and he held on to my hand for the rest of our meal.

"So, what's next?" I felt the food 'itis' begin to take over me. I had eaten too much, but it was so delicious.

"I almost forgot." D'Angelo chuckled and kissed my hand. "This food and you had me stuck. Are you ready to go?"

"I wish you would just tell me where we're going."

"Do you trust me or nawl?" My boo pouted his full lips from across the booth.

"Yeah, yeah," I whined.

"Well, let's go."

We held hands and talked about our future and the love we shared for one another. I knew you might be thinking that we were just kids but believe me when I say that we knew what love meant. Growing up in an orphanage really put our lives in prospective. We were given up as kids and lost our families. But by God's grace, we found a home, a family, and a love with one another. D'Angelo completed me! He filled my heart and made me want to do and be a better person! There was no way anyone could make me deny that. He saw what was in me even when I failed to see it for myself!

"What are we doing at Nate's Tats for Less?" I turned up my nose and glanced at D'Angelo.

"First, I'ma need for you to fix your face, love," he teased and wrapped his arms around me tightly. "And second, because it's my surprise! We gon' get matchin' tattoos!"

"You're delusional, right?" I laughed at him.

"We're underage! Ain't nobody gonna tat us right now. What? Do you have fake IDs for the both of us or something?"

"This goes back to my original question. Do you trust me or nawl?" D'Angelo nibbled on my left ear. "Nate happens to a Stanton Ave Boy, so he's hookin' us up! I told you I got you. Girl!"

"I see." I sighed and grew nervous about the tattoo. "So, what tattoo are we getting?"

"What is our anniversary date?" He looked deep into my eyes and waited for my answer.

"You know we decided it would be January 1, 2006 since it was the official day after we, well, you know! But why are you askin' me somethin' that we already agreed on?"

"It has everything to do with our tattoo." He continued to look deep into my eyes. "So, those numbers are 1-1-06. 1+1+6 = 8, and we are gonna get the Roman numeral eight on our left ring fingers. It will be a special symbol that only the two of us can share. And since we gon' be together forever, it's only right that I chose the ring finger!"

"Wow," I exclaimed with watery eyes. "I can't believe you really thought of all that. I love you, baby. That's just the sweetest thing ever."

"You can chill with that sweety shit." He joked but not really. "But I love you too, girl. I can guarantee I'ma marry you one day! I got you for life!"

"Forever, babe." I kissed him passionately. "And for always!"

***

I wished I could say that the two of us rode off into the sunset with our matchin' tats! But this wasn't a fairytale, and that was not what happened over here. The sisters were livid when they found out about our tats. One of the jealous bitches snitched on us! Those hoes were upset that D'Angelo cut them off, and I guess they thought that snitch game would break us up! Far from it though. We lost some personal privileges for a month, but the love remained. Those sluts didn't do shit but slow down my sex life for thirty days!

But on to more pressin' business. I did receive some mixed emotional news the first week of April! The sisters were able to find my Aunt Camille. I found out that she never knew I existed until she got a call, and she would love to meet me. As much as I wanted a relationship with my blood family, I noticed a change in D'Angelo's demeanor when I mentioned my news. For years, we had become one another's family, and now, I had an extension that he lacked. I was happy, but I didn't want it to be at the cost of my true love's emotions.

I met with my Aunt Camille, and we immediately hit it off. I saw so much of myself in her, and she felt likewise about me. She showed me pictures of my mother and different family members I never knew of. I had grandparents, two uncles, and several cousins. I instantly wanted to meet them all, but a part of me felt guilty about losing D'Angelo. I confessed my love to my aunt. She said she understood my feelings, but she didn't plan on losing me for another fifteen years.

It turned out that she never heard from my mother after her last attempt to contact her when I was a baby. Camille said they had fallen out back in the DR, way before my mom was sent to the states.

SANTA BABY, BRING ME A DOPE BOY FOR CHRISTMAS

There was talk of a family friend sleeping with my Aunt Camille, but Camille claimed she was a mature fifteen-year-old that was truly in love with the nineteen-year-old guy. She and my mother were very close, and she confided in my mother to keep it a secret. But my mother refused, and their parents were furious about the whole ordeal. Camille was shipped off to a boarding school, and she never forgave my mother for that betrayal.

The sisters were sorry that I was leaving, but they were equally happy that I was able to find my biological family. My roommates and other teens were in the same headspace of the sisters, but D'Angelo seemed to grow more distant with me. My heart ached for him, but he had to know that distance could never separate my love for him. I was adamant that we would still see one another. It may have not been as consistent as before, but I would always find a way back to D'Angelo.

But he wasn't tryin' to hear any of that shit! And the day I left the orphanage, I hadn't seen him at all that day. He didn't even attempt to tell me goodbye. I was more crushed than I had ever imagined, and there was no consoling me that day.

My aunt stood to her promise and brought me back to the orphanage on the weekends, just so I could find D'Angelo. But for some reason, he managed to avoid me on all my visits. I tried to call him, but after he discovered my new number, he blocked me! My sadness grew to anger after a few months of his behavior. I would rub on my tattoo and wished it would go away, along with the rest of my feelings for D'Angelo! But of course, it was permanent, as were my feelings for my true love.

I stopped going to the orphanage. I let his absence seep its way into my spirit. I did try to call Sister Sophie, but she informed me that D'Angelo got shipped off to juvie after a drive-by shooting! Thankfully, he was not harmed, but a young guy was killed in the drive-by. The cops also found drugs in the vehicle. D'Angelo was a minor, so he would be locked up until age eighteen at most. But I didn't know where they sent him, so I couldn't reach out to him.

I was able to make friends with a set of twins, Keya and Temeka. We were all in the same grade, and their mom happened to be best friends with my aunt. I was surprised at how different they were, but they were identical. Keya was more soft-spoken and caring while Temeka was more ratchet and loud! Keya had a more conservative style while Temeka loved an opportunity to twerk on a nigga! But we all agreed to attend nursing school together and remained great friends to this day. As much as I was happy to graduate high school, find my family, and attend college, there would forever be a part of me that felt incomplete because there was someone missing.

-5-

December
Sayin' I Do But I Don't

"I can't believe your special day has finally arrived, bihh!" Temeka raved and hugged me tenderly. "My other bestie is about to be a married woman!"

"Do you always have to be so extra?" Keya rolled her eyes at her twin.

"As much as humanly possible." Temeka fired back and stuck her tongue out at the two of us.

"Umm, December! Hello, are you okay, boo?"

"Yeah, December." Keya tried to read the troubled look on my face. "Are you alright, love?"

"I'm good." I lied, but I was sure Keya caught the hint. "Just wedding jitters, I guess,"

"Oh, okay." Keya gave a slight nod. "Umm, Temeka?"

"What's good?" Temeka was looking over her crimson, fitted Vera Wang bridesmaid dress in the full-length mirror. "You know what? Steven's homeboy… Trevor? Yeah, he might be the dick I hop on tonight. He's so tall and chocolatey! Not to mention, I love those sexy dreads on him too."

"That's outstanding." Keya shook her head.

"But do you think you can go check on the

SANTA BABY, BRING ME A DOPE BOY FOR rest of the CHRISTMAS

wedding party for us? You know, run a tight ship and make sure everything is runnin' smoothly."

"For sure." She gave us both air kisses and switched her hips out of the dressing room.

Keya walked over to the door, made sure her twin was out of sight, and locked the door behind her.

"Okay." Keya sighed before taking a seat next to me by the vanity set. "Now that we have the drama queen out of our hair, would you like to tell me what's really going on with you?"

"I don't know if I can go through with this!" I sobbed and tried my best not to ruin my makeup with the tissue. "I know I was confident last night, and Steven is a great guy, but I just don't know!"

Keya wrapped her arms around me, and I started glancing down at the tat on my ring finger. I couldn't help but wonder about D'Angelo. He always seemed to run across my mind more and more lately.

"You're thinkin' about him again, aren't you?" Keya pouted her lips, and I simply nodded.

"Honey, what's it gonna take to get that boy out of

your system? How many years has it been since the last time you saw him?"

"Girl," I took a few deep breaths, "it's been fourteen years and counting! God, that sounds like an eternity now that I spoke it out loud. Fourteen years and I'm still hung up over my first love. It's like I can't even put it into real words. The way things ended, it just didn't sit well with me! The way he just dropped off the face of the Earth! And I tried to go back to the orphanage to see him, but he always managed to dodge me!"

"But yet and still," Keya grabbed my left hand and ran her fingers over the symbolic tattoo, "you have never let him go in your heart. And here it is, your wedding day! Steven is an incredible and successful doctor! But you are still allowing your heart to live in the past."

"I know you're right, Keya." I felt the tears form once again in my eyes. "But I can't turn my heart on and off. He still has that special part of me! I can't deny the way I feel. I just can't!"

I felt so guilty for holding on to my love for D'Angelo. Steven was a great man, and the two of us started dating over five years ago. I was a nurse at Citizen's Hospital, and he was a medical student at that time. We exchanged glances with one another while passing through the hallways of the hospital.

After a few weeks of cat and mouse, Steven approached me with a conversation. And over time, I grew to like and love him. We had quite a few things in common. We were both in the medical field and loved helping others. He always laughed at my witty jokes, my aunt loved him, and his family embraced me with open arms.

Steven had the status and ability to make me a happy woman. Had it not been for my longing of D'Angelo; I could see the two of us starting a family and growing old together. But there was always a voice in the back of my head that warned me to rethink my marriage plans. But how could I do that or have these feelings today? Within the next few hours, I was supposed to say, "I Do," and I was feeling like I didn't want that anymore.

"Do you want to make the announcement that you don't want to get married?" Keya asked.

"Maybe I'm just getting cold feet." I lied once more but looked at myself in the full-length mirror.

If I could just get out of my head, I would appreciate all the time and effort my family and friends put into this day for me. I had a ten-thousand-dollar Vera Wang exclusive wedding dress on me. It was ivory white with a lace fit and flare style. It took over three months and several fittings just to find the perfect dress for today.

KNOCK! KNOCK!

"I forgot I locked the door. I better get that." Keya unlocked the door, and Temeka made yet another dramatic entrance.

"Tha fuck y'all heifers had goin' on in here?" Temeka snarled at the two of us. "I'ma let it slide for now! I brought the makeup artist with me because I saw you tearin' up, December! It will be okay, boo. You just got some last-minute jitters. Do you wanna hit this joint I got in my purse? It might calm your nerves a lil' bit."

"I swear you do the most." Keya snickered, and the tension was lifted momentarily.

I was happy to take a few pulls from the joint while the makeup artist beat my face once more. This was supposed to be the happiest day of my life. I had to find a way to push through it because if D'Angelo and I were meant to be, he would have never dismissed me the way he did. I had to believe that; otherwise, I would never be able to marry Steven.

"Pardon me, ladies." My Aunt Camille tapped on the dressing room door and stared in awe of my beauty. "Aww, my beautiful niece! You look so much like your mother; I wish she could be here with us. Let me stop before I mess up my makeup!"

"Please." Temeka rolled her eyes. "We are tryin' to maintain an upbeat tempo in here."

"Well…" My aunt had a withered wooden box in her hands as she took a seat beside me in the room. "I wanted to share some of our Dominican traditions with you on this special day. These are called 'Arras': symbolic wedding unity coins. These thirteen coins have been in our family for generations. Your abuela wanted to make sure you had them for your wedding day. It signifies that the couple pledges to provide for each other and that material goods are to be shared equally."

"Thank you so much, Auntie." I embraced her and glanced at the shiny golden coins filled with my heritage. "I can't wait to visit the DR and meet the rest of my family."

"Yes." Aunt Camille smiled. "They can't wait to see you. I also incorporated a few dishes from the Dominican Republic on the menu for the reception. We will have some 'Pasteles en Hoja' (tamales), 'Pernil Dominicano' (pulled pork), and for dessert, some 'Dulce de leche' (milk fudge)!"

CHRISTMAS

"Damn, now I'm hungry!" Temeka whined.

"You're the one that wanted to smoke that joint," Keya whispered in front of my aunt.

"Sounds like you have a case of the munchies, my love," Aunt Camille fired back.

"Come with me. I might can hook you up with a lil' something. Niece, you look amazing, and it's truly an honor to walk you down the aisle. I'll get out of your hair, and I'll see you by the chapel door."

"I love you, Auntie, and thanks for everything." I smiled as she headed to the door with Temeka behind her.

"Before I go," my aunt paused. "Let me bless your marriage with our Dominican Republic motto: 'Dios, Patria, Libertad'! It means 'God, Fatherhood, Liberty'! Salute,"

"Are you ready to get this show on the road, bestie?" Keya showed concern.

"I'm gonna give it my best shot." I sighed but still felt uncertain about my heart. A part of me wanted to get married to see if I could get my first love out of my system, and the other part just didn't want to spend the rest of my life alone and bitter.

"Okay, boo." Keya put on a big smile. "We're all set to go! Take a few deep breaths and know that we got you, okay?"

ADRIANNE

I did as she asked of me and placed my laced veil over my face. I decided to use the St. Francis Chapel. What better place to share my special moment? It had been years since I last spoke to any of the sisters, and I was grateful to have them share in my moment with me. Aunt Camille was waiting by the chapel door to escort me inside the church. She was dressed in a crimson and beige trimmed suit. She tried to fight back tears as we made our entrance into the lavish church. I was happy that my colleagues were able to RSVP, along with Steven's extended family and friends.

The church was draped with crimson and gold. I was always a die-hard Alabama fan, so it fit the mood for sure. I saw Steven standing tall at the alter in his black Versace tuxedo with the gold trim. Keya and Temeka wore crimson Vera Wang dresses, and the rest of my bridesmaids wore gold dresses. I felt lightheaded and unsteady, but my aunt held onto my arm while the priest began the ceremony. My mind was in a cloud of confusion and disbelief, but I plastered a wayward smile across my face. Steven mouthed the words 'I love you' while the priest addressed the crowd and the two of us.

CHRISTMAS

"Who tha fuck is doin' all that talkin' out there?" Temeka attempted to whisper, but she sucked at that. I saw her scanning the crowd, but I was unable to pinpoint the actual source.

"Meka," Keya scolded her twin, "can you please keep your voice down, and remember, we are in a church!"

"Can we please have silence from the crowd?" The priest addressed the issue head-on.

"Now, let me continue with the services! As I was saying… if anyone sees just cause for these two not to marry, can they speak now or forever hold their peace?"

"Excuse me!" Stanley, from housekeeping at Citizens' Hospital, rose to his feet. "I can't allow these shenanigans to go on! Steven, you need to speak your truth, boo!"

"WHAT THA FUCK?" Temeka fired off. "Stanley, I know you better sit yo' ratchet ass down right now! Don't make me come down there!"

Temeka commenced to remove her gold hoop earrings and flung her pumps to the side. Keya grabbed a hold of her seconds before she planned to jump on Stanley.

"December, boo, you know I love you." Stanley tried to explain. "But Steven is not the one for you, honey! He's not the one for any of you fishes!"

"THA FUCK!" Temeka took off once again and this time managed to make her way to Stanley in the pew. There were quite a few 'ohhs and awws' from the crowd, and Steven's mother collapsed from the accusation.

"What's this all about, Steven?" I pushed him repeatedly and felt the embarrassment and stares from everyone in eyeshot. "You're into men? Are you serious right now?"

"I-I..." Steven couldn't manage to get another word out before I punched him dead in his mouth.

Keya and I stomped him right at the altar, and the priest took off running along with others in the church.

"Why the fuck you didn't say anything before now, Stanley?" Temeka continued to throw blows on the man while he shrieked from the pain.

"We've been sneakin' around for the past three years," Stanley confessed, and Temeka continued to kick and punch him.

Steven tried to apologize and made a run for it through the chapel doors. Keya, Temeka, and I chased him out the church and tripped him as his tumbled down the chapel steps! We beat on him until we grew tired, and of course, the police were called. I couldn't believe the man I chose to marry had the nerve to disrespect me in that way. But I guess it was better that I found out before I went through with it.

"That sick son of a bitch!" Temeka was still fired up after all the cops and guests had escaped the madness at the church. "I never thought Steven was one of those DL brothers!"

"Tell me about it." I sighed and ate some of the reception food.

"Are you okay, December?" Keya gave me a hug and winched in pain from some of the blows we encountered.

"Yeah, girl," Temeka replied. "I thought you would be more upset about this whole situation. But you're handlin' it like a real G!"

"She was havin' cold feet anyways," Keya confessed. "She's still hung up on that other guy."

"For real, boo?" Temeka frowned. "I haven't heard you mention D'Angelo in years! And do you even know where he's at?"

"Truth," I paused. "He never left my heart, and no, I have no idea where he's at. But if I ever had the opportunity to cross paths with him again, I know I would never let him leave my side!"

"Sounds like we got a new mission on our hands." Temeka stuck out her tongue and did a twerk dance.

"There you go." Keya rolled her eyes. "I still can't believe Steven was fuckin' Stanley all those years, and none of us knew about it."

"Can we please not mention his name anymore?" I frowned and felt sick to my stomach at the thought of him.

"So, what we doin' for the rest of this weekend? It's mid-August, and our plans got changed in the most extravagant way! Let me see what's poppin'," Temeka inquired and glanced at her social media pages.

"I guess I won't be taking that honeymoon as I planned." I tried to laugh at the situation.

"Aw shit." Temeka popped her gums. "Looks like Club Velvet is throwing some birthday/tailgate party tomorrow night! I say we fall into that bitch! Are y'all game?"

"Let's do it!" I exclaimed and downed a bottle of champagne.

SANTA BABY, BRING ME A DOPE BOY FOR CHRISTMAS

-6-

D'Angelo
The Creation of 'D-Smoove'

I had been patiently waiting for my opportunity to speak my peace in this story. Please don't think I was some rotten ass nigga for the way I walked out on December years ago. But y'all had to know that December was my damn heartbeat! And knowing that she was leaving me and the life that we grew accustomed to at the orphanage, I couldn't face that shit! Yes, I was happy she found a part of her family. I was there with her the day that she read the letter from her mother; I saw the despair and anguish in her spirit. But I thought we would be together and married by the time she faced any blood relatives.

We had just made love for the very first time, and I had confessed my undying love for her. That was a moment that often haunted me, still til this day! And please know that I had been with plenty women over the past years, all different sizes, races, and quite a few cougars! But none of them ever held a candle to December! That girl was my kryptonite, no matter who I was with or how serious the relationship appeared on the outside.

When she first left, I was an absolute wreck behind it. I got in more fights, broke curfew all the time, and was focused on gettin' my paper. The sisters tried to counsel me and thought that God and therapy would allow me to see that December was given the opportunity to be with family. I was supposed to rejoice in that, and as her best friend, I should have been happy for her. But I wasn't tryin' to hear any of that shit! I guess I was just a selfish nigga! I wanted her here with me. We had never been separated since I got to St. Francis, and they just expected me to accept that shit and move forward? They could all kiss my Black ass!

So, yeah, I was in my damn feelings, and if I knew she was coming to the orphanage to see me, I stayed on ghost. I couldn't look her in the face and not shed the tears from the way she broke my heart. I couldn't allow her to see me that vulnerable! I had been there for her throughout all her pains, but I didn't want her to see me so hurt. Yes, I let my pride take over. I just thought it was safer for me to avoid her than to express the way I truly felt. I knew she was pissed or hurt, but that was how she left me. So, fuck her!

ADRIANNE

By the age of seventeen, I had gained the respect of the hood gang, Stanton Ave Boyz. Their crew ran the East side and knew how to get that paper by any means necessary. School and the legit way of gettin' money was no longer a factor in my life. I was focused on school when I had December in my life. She made me want to do better, even though those streets were constantly callin' my name. She always claimed to care about my safety and said she would die if something ever happened to me! But where was she at? She wasn't with me; she was out there livin' her best life. So, shit, I put a block on my heart and focused on the hustle game.

That same year, I was on the verge of being initiated into the crew, but us recruits had to prove ourselves to the OGs. Four of us were chosen by the homies to rob our enemies, Crutchfield Playaz, crack spot. I was ready for action, but the others were full of nerves that night. Lil Rob, one of the newbies, was coked up and jittery as fuck. But Kyle and Ricus were quiet for most of the ride to the West side. It was supposed to be an easy treat because our crew managed to pay a few fiends to leave the back door unlocked. Them Playaz installed a smokeroom for the smokers in the back of the shack. Their leader, Crazy J, felt like it brought less attention if the fiends smoked there instead of being spotted by the cops leavin' their place in a hasty manner. I did respect the way he approached it because for all the cops knew, some of the fiends could've been just hangin' around. The place didn't give a crack house vibe. It was fronted by a barbershop/food joint. If you rode past it, you wouldn't assume drugs were sold in it.

Of course, they had cameras on all angles, but we already knew where all of them were positioned. Niggas were crazy to trust geekers. They were always lookin' for money to support their next high. They didn't have any real loyalty. We pulled across the street from the spot after eleven that night. Since they sold food, the place didn't close on the weekends until after midnight. It was packed for a Friday night, and we were dressed plain with hoodies. We walked around the back, the entrance way for the geekers, and saw our informant by the gate.

Samson wiped the snot from his nose, and I gave him a head nod as he tapped on the entrance and spoke to one of the Playaz. He made small talk and allowed Lil' Rob and I to enter the establishment without a second look. The other two newbies remained in the car as lookouts. Once we got the bread, they would shoot up the spot if things went left. There was only one guy holding the money pot, but he was strapped. The dumb nigga had his piece on the table, such a sucker move! I guess things ran smooth, and he never had a reason to keep it on him. Them geekers only cared about getting' high, so they had no reason to get hostile as long as he had what they needed.

Samson got his rock, and I was next in the line. I asked for two rocks and pretended to fumble for my cash while Lil Rob stumbled his ass behind the dude. When I pretended to hand him the money, Rob stabbed him three times in his spine. While he howled in pain, I swatted his piece out of his reach and pointed my Glock directly in his face. I grabbed the stacks of cash and popped one in his skull before we took off running to the car.

I had such an adrenaline rush from what had just transpired and beat on the hood of the 1983 Impala, so we could drive off. I cheered at our accomplishment, but after a block of drivin' off, we noticed the Playaz were on our tail. Ricus was driving like a madman, and I was firin' off shots from the passenger side. We had made it to the interstate exit, and the traffic was hectic that night. We swerved through lanes and almost smacked a few cars but saw the light when our exit was soon approaching us. As Ricus made the exit turn, we saw an ambush of Crutchfield Playaz cocked and ready for us.

Ultimately, Ricus hit the side of someone's house while he lost control of the wheel. The Impala was rattled with bullets, and the police were also in pursuit. Long story short, three of us were arrested for reckless endangerment, drugs, and an unregistered firearm in the car. Lil' Rob was killed from the impact of the wreck. Being that we were all minors, they shipped our asses to Youngstown Detention Center. The prosecutors offered us a few deals, but I wasn't no damn snitch! They knew it was gang related because of the shooting that happened at the Crutchfield Playaz spot, but I threw that burner, the one that I used to kill their homie, out the window. So, the law had no direct way to tie that shit to us.

I did my time in there, but my mind always drifted back to December. I tried my best to hate her and replace her with countless women, but it couldn't be done. I even found myself callin' out her name during sex! How pathetic was that? She was like some type of virus that had no cure. She was my rider and the only woman that owned my heart, and without her, it never seemed to beat the same.

After my release from the detention center, I was a hungry eighteen-year-old with the respect from the Stanton Ave Boyz. They knew about the offers that were given, but there was no snitchin' in my DNA. The OGs spared no expense on my release, and I was welcomed with open arms into their family. My only request was for them to welcome my homie, Figga. Me and him grew tight over my time locked away. He had a lot of hustle in him, and I needed someone I could trust to have my back in any situation. After six months on the street, the two of us managed to secure an apartment and had a few hoopties for transportation. Figga was more of the heartbreaker and flashy dude. His six foot four, muscular build, and dark chocolate skin drove them hoes insane. He had the gift of gab and the heart of a street savage. I was more lowkey with my moves. I was always guarded, thanks to December, but after a few blunts, I mellowed out.

Chicks loved my milk chocolate skin, deep dimples, platinum bottom grill, and fade. I used to rock dreads in my teen years, but after I was locked up, I didn't have anyone to care for them. Not to mention, I looked just as handsome without them. Women loved my hazel eyes and shy guy demeanor. I spent most of my time gettin' approached and not vice versa. I stood six foot two, slender with muscles, and always with a fitted cap and diamond earrings.

My hustle game really hit its peak in my twenties. There were a few run-ins with the Crutchfield Playaz over that decade. But when they attempted to hit us, we always came back the victorious crew. Me and Figga ended up starting a car detailing shop on their end of town. After a few shootouts and conversations from both sides, they decided to leave that alone. The business was profitable and didn't interfere with their dope game. Or that was what we wanted them to think! We had connections on both ends of town but were able to make transactions in the shop without them knowing about it.

This was just another accolade that made me an asset to the Stanton Ave Boyz. The fact that I was smoove enough to step on enemy turf, make money, and live to see another day spoke volumes for my credibility, and I was given my own crew and spot to run for them. Figga was my right hand on everything I touched, and together, we were a success. I was happy that I had everything that money could buy, and my life was on easy street. But my happiness was always haunted by the loss of December. I always told her that I would become the king on the streets, and she was supposed to be my queen. So many years had passed, and I wondered if she still thought about me.

So, yeah, the name 'D Smoove' evolved from my hustle game and all the money I was able to accumulate in the process. D'Angelo was the young boy that wanted to get it. He was the lovesick boy that invested his heart into a girl that left him on red. But D Smoove was a man with that paper. He locked his heart away and swallowed the key to it. The streets were his heart, and the bitches were just pieces on a board game.

"D!" I was halted from my trip down memory lane by the voice of my homie, Figga.

"Nigga, you ain't heard a word I said to your ass!"

"Boy, you wild!" I chuckled nervously and ran my left hand over my hair waves. He knew I did that shit whenever I spaced out on him.

"Yeah, that's what I thought." He laughed heartily and sparked a blunt. "What's up with you, bruh? I mean, you always fade out on me, but lately, it seems to happen on the regular! Do we got some beef with a nigga? Just speak on it, bruh!"

"Calm down, bruh." I fanned my homie, but I loved the way he rocked with me. "It's nothin' like that. Plus, you already know what time it is! If there was any issue on these streets, I'd let you know about it."

"So, what is it?" He shrugged his shoulder and took a gulp of his Corona beer. "Spill that shit! You know we always keep it a buck between us."

"It's really nothin'." I rubbed my hands together nervously and glanced at my ring finger. I had thought about covering up that Roman numeral eight tat on my finger. My body was full of tats nowadays. They were all over my hands and body but nothing on my face. But no matter the tat, that finger tat was always the one that seemed to stand out for me.

"You thinkin' about December, huh?" Figga asked and gave a slight chuckle. "I don't know why you keep torturin' yourself like this, bruh. You went through all the trouble of finding her social media pages, and you know where she works! Why don't you just pop up on her and end all this madness?"

"You just doin' a lot of talkin'." I felt my palms sweat from the thought of being face to face with December. "I just wanted to see what she was about on there. You know, was she being a thot or the good girl that I was used to. She seems happy with that dude that she tags in some of her pics, so I'ma just fall back and stay in my lane."

"Are you believin' the bullshit that you're tryin' to feed me?" Figga mocked me. "You have been tellin' me for years about that damn girl. And you have all the cards on your side, but instead of closing the gap between you two, you wanna just fall back? If that was the case, why did you even look her up online? Why torture yourself like that?"

I was just on the verge of responding when I received a phone call from my latest bitch, Willandra.

"Fuck." I sighed in agony. I had forgotten that I was supposed to pick her whining ass up from the nail shop earlier. I had been at Figga's crib for the past couple hours, but Willandra asked me to get her over an hour ago. I knew she was about to cuss my ass out for that shit. I went ahead and answered her call. "I already know you mad, so please don't holler in my damn ear!"

"Really, D!" She whined, and she knew I hated that shit. "You just get around yo' nigga and forget all about me?"

"I was just caught up over here with the homie," I replied honestly. "I do apologize. I can burn out of here right now and get you."

"Did you really think I was gonna stand around for a whole hour and wait around on you?" she spat. "I called an Uber and went home. I had to be here to pick up Angel from my momma."

"Aw, okay," I replied. Angel was Willandra's daughter from a previous relationship. She was a bubbly little three-year-old. Although she wasn't mine, I spared no expense on her when I was around. She managed to find her way into my heart. Her mother, on the other hand, was a piece of work.

Although Willandra was beautiful, she was also sneaky and very jealous hearted. She stood five-foot-three, mixed with Puerto Rican and Black, and had a Coke-bottle shape that Nicki Minaj couldn't pull off! She always rocked a short hair bob and her cat-like grey eyes were a definite weakness for any man. I caught her in a few lies about niggas, but then again, I never told her I loved her. As far as I was concerned, she could do what she wanted because I always did! But if she heard about or saw a chick in my face, she was always ready to fight that chick.

"Is that all you gotta say to me?" she continued.

"I said I was sorry, girl." I got irritated. "What else do you want from me?"

"Sounds like you got some makin' up to do." She snickered, and I knew she wanted this dick and a few bands. I would have given it to her anyway because her crazy ass had some bomb ass sex.

"I'm on tha job." I nodded and confirmed her implementation.

"Well, I gotta tend to my baby girl, but I guess I will be seein' you a little later?"

"I got you, girl."

I was glad for the distraction, but after I ended the call with my chick, Figga was still waitin' on a response from our conversation.

"I'm still waiting, bruh." He smiled.

"Go on with all that shit." I fanned him away and helped myself to one of his beers in the fridge.

"You need to go see December and stop playin'," Figga spat out. "If you want, we can roll through together. Whatever it takes to get your head back in the game."

"Head back in the game?" I snarled. "What's that supposed to mean?"

"You just not as focused as you used to be." My homie shrugged his shoulders once more. "I just think that you would feel a lot better if you just got out yo' feelings and made a move! If things are solid with her and her dude, seein' you shouldn't stop anything!"

"She probably doesn't want to see me anyways." I sighed and rubbed my hair waves nervously. "The way I did her years ago, she's bound to hate my ass by now. Nawl, I don't wanna get hurt all over again. I'm good with Willandra. At least I know what it is with that crazy girl."

"That bitch needs to be put in a fuckin' straitjacket." Figga clowned. "The way she attacked them girls at the club last week! If we weren't cool with the owner, we would have gotten banned from there!"

"Say less, bruh." I laughed heartily.

"Just because the chicks bought us drinks," Figga shook his head, "she assumed you was fuckin' one of them and attacked all three of them hoes!"

"I'm done going to clubs with her stupid ass!" I clowned with him.

"So, how are you gonna keep her from my birthday party tomorrow?"

"That was too easy." I smiled sneakily. "You know she's banned from Club Velvet!"

"I wondered why you picked that club." Figga fell out. "You one sneaky muthafucka!"

"I can be." I gave him a pound. "They even got her pictures on the door. She's not even allowed in the damn parking lot. But don't worry, I paid for a weekend resort for her and her crew. They will be leaving out late tonight and won't be back until Sunday afternoon. So, we gon have a great and stress-free night!"

"I'm all for that," he acknowledged.

"Well, let me break out of here." I dapped up my homie and stood to my feet. "I got some pussy to eat and pound, so I can make sure we have a peaceful party and weekend!"

-7-

D'Angelo
Put On a Smile

I can pretend when I'm out with my friends
I ain't thinkin' about you
I can pretend like I ain't in my feelings
But that ain't true, nah (nah)
When I called you out your name
That was my ego, my plan and pain
I should be a movie star
The way I play the part
Like everything's okay
Oh, not tryna be the life of the party
Oh, not that, just for everybody
But it's all just a knack
That I can't have you back
Without you runnin', goin' crazy
(Chorus): Tryna put on a smile (put on a smile)
Tryna fight these tears from cryin'
But Lord knows I'm dyin' dyin'....'

I cruised the streets and puffed on my Kush while I listened to the sounds of Silk Sonic. Most niggas didn't know I was really an R&B type dude. When I thought about December or needed to get focused, I synced some songs from YouTube to the sound system in my Range. This particular song described the exact way I felt about her and the way I let my pride get in the way.

It was the night of Figga's birthday bash, and we had made announcements on social media, the radio, and word of mouth. Everybody who was anybody planned to turn up with yo' boy. We were both officially in our dirty thirties! I was happy about my success, but I had thought I would be married to December with a few babies by now.

I'm tired of thinkin' about her! I thought to myself while the music played. *I'ma get wasted tonight and find me a chick to fuck on tonight!*

I knew that sounded immature, but I was tired of the way I was feeling. I knew that once I got a few drinks in my system, I would be free from the pain in my chest. Even if it was a temporary fix, I would take what I could get! It was almost eleven at night, and the parking lot was packed at Club Velvet. I had secured the night by sending Willandra off to a resort. She was upset that she couldn't be at the party, but after I dicked her down a few times, I didn't hear too much more about it. I looked forward to a peaceful night and a great time. But there was something missin'. I just couldn't shake that shit.

I pulled my pearl coated, 2020 Range Rover into the reserved parking area of the club. Figga was already in the lot with the rest of the Boyz. He made his way to my ride once he saw me kill my engine. He tapped on the passenger side window, and I unlocked the door for him.

"I'm tha birthday boy, so let's turn up." Figga pounded me up and pulled out a pack of cigars. "I pre-rolled for us tonight. We gon get fucked up! Did you see the crowd? And damn, these hoes are lookin' right tonight."

"Thanks, bruh." I fired up one of the blunts. I was already in the zone after the blunt I smoked on the way there. "Yeah, the city really showed some love tonight. I saw some definite dimes in the entrance doors."

"I'm just glad you got rid of that crazy bitch." Figga clowned. "Now I know it's gonna be a party! I seen a set of twins in the parking lot. I wouldn't mind having both tonight!"

"You know you wild." I dapped up my homie, but I knew he was serious about that last remark. "Hey, maybe we can both smash one or both. Some twins are into that type of shit!"

"It's my birthday." He shrugged his shoulders and smiled. "It's whatever tonight. You ready to head on in there? We just been vibin' outside while we waited on you."

"Let's do this!"

***

After two hours of drinks, Kush, and great music, yo' boy was on cloud nine! There was nothin' and no one on my mind, only the vibe and the love from the crowd. Our VIP section was gated off from the rest of the club. There was mirror tint on the encased windows, so it was really whatever in there!

"How you feelin', bruh?" Figga grabbed me for a brief hug.

"I'm doin' great." I laid my head back on the plush velvet loveseat in the room. A ratchet bitch was on her knees, givin' me some deep throat. I spotted her close to the VIP area, opened the door, and gave her a head nod. She knew what time it was after I furnished her with a few lines of coke. It wasn't my drug of choice, but I knew some bitches liked to use it, and it made them freakier. I was about to cum, and I felt the chick gag on my shit. I had a full nine inches of thick dick. And the way she handled my shit made me want to bend her over, but my peeps were in the room. Plus, I didn't know that bitch! Head was a different story. "I'm bout to bust. Are you gonna catch it, bihh?"

She nodded and played with my balls while she swallowed my seeds. The adrenaline rush was exactly what I needed. I kissed her on the top of her head and allowed her access to the food and drink bar after she cleaned up her face.

"I was thinkin' about steppin' to one of them twins." Figga fired up a blunt from his pack. "I saw them and their homegirl by the bar. The one, Temeka, she's feisty, just the way I like 'um. I could definitely do some things with her and that smart mouth."

"So, she's one of those?" I clowned. "She sounds like Willandra's crazy ass! The crazy ones always have the best pussy, bruh."

"Nawl, man." Figga joked. "That nut case is one in a million. Plus, Temeka just seems to flirt with an attitude. It doesn't mean she's like that all the time. But I was gonna head back over that way. Why don't you get out of this room and come with me? You might like the other twin; I forgot her name though. Not to mention, they got another girl with them. Now, she's the one I really wanted, but Temeka walked over to me first."

"I see." I took a deep breath, a swig of Hennessy, and gave a sigh. "It's a real nigga's birthday celebration. Let's do this, bruh."

I grabbed my Dolce & Gabbana, black sunglasses to hide my red eyes, tipped my hat to the ratchet bitch, and emerged into the crowd with my homie by my side. We had to elbow our way to the bar because the crowd was so thick. But I immediately noticed the attraction my homie had to the twins. They were caramel and full-figured goddesses. The one with more sass, that Figga locked on, was wearing a tight blue mini with pumps to match. Her twin had a long ponytail and sported a green and gold jumpsuit. I looked for another chick with them, but there was just an empty seat.

"This is my bruh, D Smoove." Figga made my introduction, and I gave them a head nod.

"Hello, ladies." I smiled with my grill and licked my full lips. "I hope you all are enjoying yourselves tonight."

"Hell yeah!" Temeka swayed her body to the music and gave Figga a sexy wink. "I'm so glad I convinced my sistas to come out tonight. We had a ruff day yesterday! This was just what we needed."

"Hush it up, Meka!" Her twin scolded her.

"Stop gettin' fucked up and tellin' everybody's business!"

"It's not like that, is it?" I smiled and raised an eyebrow. "As fine as y'all are, I just know it had something to do with a weak ass nigga."

"You have no idea." Temeka joked and continued to sway to the beat.

"Uggh." Her twin popped her gums and rolled her eyes. "I just can't with you. I'm bout to go check on sis. You trippin'!"

She rose to her feet and soon disappeared into the crowd while Temeka discussed a disastrous wedding from the day before. I never thought I would hear a story like that one! Her sister found out her hubby-to-be was an undercover brother! Damn, now that was some bullshit.

"I feel sorry for your sister." I shook my head in disbelief. "I gotta invite y'all to the VIP room. Where is she at?"

"They headed this way now!" Temeka pointed while I waited for them to approach us.

"Took y'all heifers long enough. Are you good, sis?"

I turned around to introduce myself to the failed bride, but my heart skipped a beat when I saw the vision in front of me.

"Hey, guys." Temeka began to slur her words, and I felt like my heart was gonna beat outside of my chest. "This is our other sister, our best friend, December!"

December was still the sexy vision that she'd been in her teens. She wore an all-black, Gucci romper with gold stilettos. Her curves had my man at attention, and her hair curled down her back with an auburn tint. She tried to steady her movements and waved at us with a goofy smile. I had never seen December intoxicated, and I didn't like that shit. A part of me wanted to drag her out of here and scold her, but I remained quiet and studied her body. I wanted to rip those clothes off her back and remind her of why she fell so hard for me. But I also wondered if she recognized me behind these shades.

"Did you say December?" Figga smiled and glanced over at me.

"Yeah." Temeka rolled her neck.

CHRISTMAS

"Nice to meet you all." December chuckled and eased her way onto the bar stool. "This is a great party. What are your names?"

"Oh, I'm Figga," He answered and kissed her hand gently. I immediately clenched my jaws but tried to not show my anger. "And this is my bruh, D Smoove!"

"D Smoove?" December laughed. "I know that's not your government name! I gave you a real name, and y'all got these hood names for me."

"Well, shawty," Figga replied. "The hood calls me Figga, but my real name is Josh."

"And what about you, D Smoove?" She gave me a look, and I thought that maybe she was sizing me up or curious about me.

"They say I'm the smoothest nigga in these streets." I exhaled and removed my glasses from my face. The look of disbelief in her eyes told me that she was in shock. "But the 'D' stands for D'Angelo!"

"Oh, my God!" December shrieked and placed her hands on both sides of her face.

"So, are you the one that got my girl's mind gone? Her long lost love and all that?" Temeka cheered as if December really kept me relevant in her life.

95

"I didn't know I still had that effect." I stared deep into December's orbs, and I noticed the tears form in her eyes. "How you been, DeeDee?"

-8-

December
Rewrite the Stars

"Oh my God!" I shrieked and immediately felt lightheaded from the shock and amount of liquor I had consumed for the evening.

For the past fourteen years, I had dreamt of nothing more than to be face to face with D'Angelo. To ask him why he left me on red and crushed my soul and tell him that no one ever filled his place in my heart. Besides the haircut, he was still the slender, milk chocolate God that captured my heart years ago. I felt the tears well up in my eyes as he stared through to my soul. I felt anxious, boxed in, and in absolute shock.

"I didn't know I still had that effect on her." D'Angelo laughed heartily and licked his full lips. I remembered the way they felt against my skin and felt my kitty become moist. "How you been, DeeDee?"

"Who did he just say?" Temeka popped her gums and glanced at our circle. "DeeDee, where did that come from?"

"Just a little nickname I had for my bestie." D'Angelo smiled and wiped one of my tears away with his thumb. I felt my body vibrate from his touch. And as much as I wanted to run into his arms, there was a part of me that wanted to run away from him. "She used to call me Gelo!"

"Aww." Temeka cackled along with the rest of them. "Y'all was all cute and shit! Damn, sis, you forgot to mention that part, didn't you?"

Suddenly, my tears of joy were replaced with thoughts of anger and despair.

How could he just stand there and smile when he knows how deeply he hurt me? Those thoughts rang through my head while I observed only laughs and smiles from my circle of friends. *He didn't even give me the opportunity to say goodbye! He just allowed me to suffer and go about his life! Did D'Angelo ever really love me?*

"HOW DARE YOU?" I screamed above the crowded party and loud music. It caused a slight hush from my friends. I balled up my fists and felt the perspiration on my palms.

"Who are you screamin' at like that, DeeDee?" D'Angelo raised his brow and approached my face with a few steps. He attempted to stroke my face once more, but I dodged his advances and slapped him hard across the face.

"YOU'RE JUST GONNA STAND THERE AND ACT LIKE THE WAY YOU LEFT ME WAS COOL, HUH? YOU JUST WANT ME TO PRETEND THAT MY HEART DIDN'T BREAK BECAUSE YOU NEVER GAVE ME THE OPPORTUNITY TO SAY GOODBYE! I LOVED YOU MORE THAN ANYTHING, AND YOU JUST TURNED YOUR BACK ON ME! FUCK YOU, D'ANGELO! I'M OUT THIS BITCH!"

I grabbed my clutch purse and hauled ass to the nearest exit of the club. I allowed the cool and crisp Alabama air to invade my lungs and exhaled some of the hatred encased in my heart. I also felt my head begin to spin as I noticed D'Angelo scanning the parking lot for me.

"December!" He hollered and looked through a row of vehicles. "Please don't be like this! Can we at least talk please?"

I had to call an Uber because I was in no condition to drive myself home. I pulled out my iPhone 13 Pro and accessed the Uber app. I had to wait an additional twenty minutes for my ride and manage to hide from the man I loved.

"December." D'Angelo snuck up from behind and placed his big hands across my shoulders. I attempted to jerk away from his grasp, but he easily overpowered me. "Please don't be like this!"

"Let go of me, D'Angelo or D Smoove! Whatever you are callin' yourself these days! I don't know who you are, and maybe I never did! I thought the love that we shared was so real, and I allowed it to cloud my judgement and even my failed marriage! Did you know, that on my wedding day, all I could think about was YOUR ass? I still pictured the two of us walking down the aisle and havin' a few babies! But you threw my love away years ago, right? You knew I was leaving the orphanage and just erased me! You dodged all my visits, and you blocked my calls! So, tell me something. What was it for? Why lie about the way you felt? Why get these fuckin' tats? What was the purpose for any of it?"

I felt the tears streaming down my face like a river. I felt a wave of relief that swept across my spirit. I had kept those words and emotions tucked away for so long. I needed to get that out of my system. I needed to be able to speak my truth to the man that crippled me emotionally. D'Angelo had managed to hold me in his arms while I cried my eyes out. I took a few deep breaths and pushed away from his embrace. As I glanced upon his face, I noticed the trail of tears that flowed from his eyes.

"It was never over for me." He sobbed and reached out his hands for me. "It still ain't over!"

He pulled me close to him and placed his hands on either side of my face. He had me in his trance, and I allowed him to kiss me long and passionately. It was as if the rest of the world stood still, and the two of us were encased inside of a kiss that would last a lifetime.

"Umm, excuse me!" Temeka tapped me on the shoulder, and D'Angelo released his lips from mine. "What the fuck was all those dramatics about in there, sis? I mean, you slapped the fire outta that nigga, and now you out here sharin' spit with him?"

"I don't care what it was about." His homie, Figga, clapped his hands and smiled. "I'm just glad he found you again. He ain't been focused on shit lately, and I knew that you could get him back on his square, December! That nigga is still sprung on you."

"Seriously." I wiped my eyes and glanced over at D'Angelo. He spoke no words, but his eyes revealed his truth. "Is that how you feel?"

"It must be true, sis." Keya smiled and gave a head nod. "You got your boy over there speechless!"

"I just can't believe I found you again." D'Angelo scanned my body and drew me back into his arms for a great big hug. I had dreamed of this moment for so long, and I wanted to enjoy it for the rest of our lives.

***

Since the day we rekindled our connection at that club, we stayed in constant contact with one another. It was just like old times; only, we didn't have to sneak around from the sisters in the orphanage. I didn't hesitate to give my true love a sample of my ripened goodies. He was still the only one to make my body quake from his monster, and he sent my body on a rollercoaster ride every time. But although I was happy to have him back in my life, I felt uneasy about the psycho bitch that refused to leave him alone.

Willandra was like a thorn in our side. He repeatedly tried to end things with her, but she called and showed up at his crib on the regular. There were a few occasions that me and the girls had to fight it out with her. She showed up at restaurants a few times when the two of us were just trying to vibe with one another. She told me it would always be 'on sight' and that I needed to watch my back! I wasn't the type to back down from a fight, but after some time, the shit grew old and tiresome. We both decided to block her from all social media, and D'Angelo switched up his routine and whips to avoid her.

I knew that D'Angelo was a real catch on these streets, so any hungry chick would jump at the chance to be with him. But he mentioned that his heart only belonged to me and that he never confessed his love for anyone else. Even though I attempted to marry Steven a few months ago, D'Angelo was the only man for me. Being with him again allowed me to confirm those feelings completely.

"What are you thinkin' about, love?" D'Angelo showered me with kisses on the back of my neck while he placed his hands around my thick waist. "I just can't seem to keep my hands off you, girl. I love you so much, babe."

"Just thinkin' about your stalker." I took a deep breath and turned to face my soulmate. I saw his smile fade, and a few aggravated lines emerged on his brow. "She's never gonna allow us to be happy, babe. And I'm tired of fightin' her ass every time I see her ass! Not only that, but it's also not safe for me to keep fightin' her like that!"

"I know what you mean, babe." D'Angelo gave a slight pause and stared into my glowing face. "Rewind that last part. You said it's no longer safe for you to be fightin' that bitch. What you mean exactly?"

"It means," I smiled heartily and placed his hand on my heart and then stomach, "I have a greater part of me that needs to be protected at all costs. I just found out the other day, baby. We are expecting, and I hope you are okay with that."

"ARE YOU KIDDIN' ME RIGHT NOW?" D'Angelo jumped for joy and spun me around a few times. "My baby is havin' my baby! This is the second-best news I could ever receive in my life!"

"I'm so glad to hear you say that!" We embraced once more and sealed it with a kiss. "But why did you say it was the second-best thing? This is the best thing in my life right now! Well, of course, you played a major part of it. But having a baby, that's always been a dream of mine. And the fact that the child is with the only man I ever loved, that's the peak for me."

"I didn't mean anything negative by that, baby." He showed his deep dimples and glanced down at his vibrating phone. "I just meant that makin' you my wife was always at the top of the list for me."

"Aw, babe." I grabbed him by his neck and stuck my tongue down his throat. "It's always going to be a 'yes' for me! I never wanna lose us again. It's forever for me!"

"Always, babe," D'Angelo replied but looked worried as he looked into his phone.

"What's going on?" I frowned. "Is everything okay?"

"I'm not sure, boo." He nervously ran his hand across his deep waves. "I gotta burn out for a minute. But when I get back, we will discuss our baby and nuptials."

"I love you, baby." I searched his face and gave him a peck on the cheek.

"Always and forever, babe."

-9-

D'Angelo
When the Bough Breaks

I was ecstatic about the news of a baby with December! These past months with her had been some of the best days of my life. Makin' love to her was the most magnetic field I had ever crossed. She was the only one to complete me and make me feel whole again. Since she was back in my life, I intended to keep her there for the rest of my life. I had to call some of my randoms and let them know that our hookups were dead! A few of them were in their feelings, but they accepted their roles. Willandra wasn't goin' for any of that shit!

That bitch refused to accept the fact that we were over! I went out my way to soothe her to the best of my abilities. The home she resided in, I paid it off for her! I also laced her with some ends to make sure her and Angel were straight. I went above and beyond to tell her that I always cared, but we just weren't meant to be together.

SANTA BABY, BRING ME A DOPE BOY FOR CHRISTMAS

She cussed, screamed, and vandalized a lot of my shit. I had the money to replace everything, but the way she kept runnin' up on December, that shit wasn't cool at all. She must've had a tracker on my phone or some shit because she stayed showing up on us when we went on dates. December wasn't an easy win, so she didn't back down from Willandra. I thought that caught her by surprise because she was so used to bitches bowin' down to her. But no matter what I tried, Willandra always seemed to pop up and start some bullshit!

Today wasn't any different, and it was a distraction from my joy of the new baby.

"Is everything okay, babe?" December frowned and ran her gentle hand across my worried face. "Do you wanna talk about it?"

"I got a few things I need to handle." I sighed, but I was sure she read through my façade.

"It shouldn't take me too long to handle. And when I get back, we can discuss the baby and our future nuptials."

"I love you, babe!" She gave me a peck on the cheek. I knew she was worried, but I didn't want to upset her. She was carryin' my seed, and I didn't want her stressed out for the baby's sake.

"Always and forever, babe." I walked away from her and headed to my Range in the driveway.

Figga had hit me up a few times about problems at the detail shop. We were convinced that Willandra managed to fuck with the water system, cut some wires, and caused her usual chaos. I assured my homie that I would handle her, but I was almost out of ideas when it came to her. I had my number changed and blocked my number before I called her line.

"WHY DO YOU KEEP FUCKIN' WITH ME?" I hollered while I drove to my next destination. "I'VE GIVEN YOU EVERYTHING YOU NEEDED, BUT YOU'RE STILL TRYIN' TO FUCK WITH MY LIFE! WHY CAN'T YOU JUST FALL THE FUCK BACK?"

"Silly rabbit." She cackled uncontrollably. "I told you once before that this thing between us ain't over until I say so! You think you can just buy me off? You think I didn't invest my feelings into this shit with you?"

"Look." I sighed and pulled into my three-car garage. "I told you that I would always care about you, and that's real. But we aren't gonna be together on the level that you want, not anymore. All this chaos and bullshit just makes you look crazy and desperate! Chill the fuck out and stop all this madness!"

"Chill the fuck out?" She laughed once more.

"Seems like you are the one that needs to wake up and chill! You send me on a heartfelt retreat one weekend, then when I return, you tell me that things are over! Like, who the fuck does that to somebody? Especially someone that has been rockin' with you for the past two years! That bitch, December, was nowhere to be found, but I was right by your side! Yeah, I got a little aggravated when I saw a bitch in yo' face! But you was never just a FUCK for me, Smoove! I had real feelings for your sorry ass! And you just expect me to walk away like it was nothing? For a bitch that cancelled you out years ago!"

"Stop callin' her that!" I raged through clenched teeth. "Don't blame her for any of this! This is all on me. I was the one that walked away from you! Stop comin' for December, and I mean that shit! Don't test me like that. You know what's up!"

"Are you really threatening me because of that BITCH?" She hollered. "Nigga, I could end that bitch in a fuckin' heartbeat if I really wanted to! You know what it is with me too, boo! I just been slappin' her around and playin' with her snobby ass! But if you really wanna test me, I can take it there! Is that what you want?"

"I said what I said." I flexed my muscles and felt the rage in my heart. "Whatever beef is with me, not her! But I'm tellin' you to back off because there will never be anything between us again. Don't get off into gangsta shit, shawty! Fall the fuck back and leave this shit alone!"

"And I said what I said, nigga!" She mocked my serious tone. "Either you get rid of that bitch, or I will! Later, babes!"

She hung up the line, and I immediately wanted to confront that hoe. But maybe that was her plan all along, to have me cornered at her crib and on her own turf. I wasn't a dumb nigga by any means, but I was concerned about the welfare of my lady and baby. Willandra was crazy enough to attempt some foul shit. She had showed me that over the years. I wasn't scared of her ass, but I didn't want her to harm December. I had to protect her at all costs just like I did when we were kids.

***

I advised December to file a restraining order against Willandra. She held out for over a week, but after I begged her and mentioned our baby, she eventually grew keen to the idea. I upped the security at my businesses and put my home up on the market. December was more than willing to have me stay at her place until we found the perfect home together. As a precaution, I had a few of my boys keep watch of her house 24/7 and installed a better security system to the place.

I enjoyed meeting December's aunt and spending more time with her crazy friends, the twins. We formally announced the new bundle to close family and friends. It was the month of December, and I wanted to plan something special for my girl on her approaching birthday.

"I love you so much, babe." December cooed on my chest after one of our many love sessions. "I never thought I could be this happy again."

"I feel the same way, babe." I ran my hand down her lower back and kissed her gently on the top of her head. "There's no place I'd rather be than here with you. It's like we were never apart all those years! Our love just picked up, right where we left it."

"Have you had anymore run ins with that crazy bitch?" December laid her naked body on top of mine and stared into my eyes.

"Why do you gotta ruin the afterglow like that?" I frowned and playfully pushed her off my semi-hardened member. "Please don't spoil the vibe by discussin' that bitch today."

"It was a fair question." She shrugged her shoulders and sat up in the bed. "You have gone through so many lengths to keep us safe lately. I was just hoping that all of these drastic measures were paying off."

"So far, so good." I nodded and watched a smile emerge on her face. "What do you have planned for later tonight, babe? I need to handle some business, but I'll be back."

"I gotta get ready for work today, but I'm off the rest of the weekend." She stretched and yawned from our heated sex session. "I guess I will see what the twins are doing since you plan on leavin' me."

"Don't say it like that, babe." I picked her up and invaded her mouth with my tongue. "I will always come back to you. You know that. I'm just glad you won't be home alone. Willandra has chilled out, but until I know she's done, I'd rather have you around people."

"Do you think she knows where I live?" December raised her brow.

"She's bound to notice that I moved," I replied. "So, I'm sure she's been trying to figure out my movements and yours."

"She's never been by here that I know of," December stated calmly. "Not to mention, you have some of your crew outside of my place around the clock."

"I just want to keep the two of you safe." I kissed her sweet lips and ran my hand across her stomach. "If something was to happen to either one of you because of that bitch, I don't know what I would do."

"We gon be alright." She wiggled her way from my grasp and entered the master bathroom.

"I'm gonna hop in this shower. I hope you managed to save some of the hot water. You know how you do!"

I watched the love of my life turn on the water and soon disappear behind the shower curtain. I was pleased to see a vision of peace across her face, but I wasn't so convinced yet. Willandra was a manipulative and connivin' bitch. She was like a rabid dog on the loose, and I never knew when she would strike again. I knew she had been served with that restraining order by now, but I had yet to hear from her. Was it possible that she was getting' the hint, or was she just waiting for a better time to

113

strike? I fired up a blunt, got dressed, and exited the house. So many thoughts ran across my mind as I made my way to Figga's residence.

-10-

Willandra
Playin' for Keeps

"I shouldn't be out all night, Mami." I whined when my mother complained about babysitting my daughter. "You act like I ask you to babysit your own granddaughter on the regular! Why are you comin' at me like that? You never have a problem watchin' all of Junior or Amelia's rugrats!"

"Don't take it like that, Willie." My mother tried to smooth things over while I grabbed my purse and winter coat from the kitchen. "I love all of my grandkids. I just planned on steppin' out tonight, and I wanted to know what time you would be back."

"Yeah, right." I frowned and made my way to her kitchen door. "I won't be gone that long. I just needed to run a few errands and go by the mall. Christmas is coming up, and I wanted to make sure I had everything I needed for Angel this year."

The cold breeze chilled my bones, and I allowed my Lexus Coupe to warm up before I exited the driveway. I did need to finish Christmas shopping, but that was not on my agenda for today. Smoove had me fucked up if he thought I was just gonna walk away from his ass! That nigga was a cash cow, and a bitch like me never intended on working or livin' below my required standards. Was that bitch's pussy lined with gold? What was her hold over him?

I was also pissed to be served with papers for a restraining order! The nerve of that bitch to feel threatened by me and go to the cops about it! That shit was just a piece of paper to me. I would still smash her ass if I saw her! I wasn't scared of going to jail, and I was never the type to back down from something I wanted! She really added more fuel to the fire, but I had to stay focused.

I had driven past Smoove's house a few times, but after working up the courage to make it into his yard and front windows, it appeared as though he moved out, like that would stop me from finding him! Did he think I was an amateur? I didn't have an eye on many of his hangouts; he did a good job of keeping that lowkey. But when we were fuckin' around, I never had the desire to know all of his whereabouts. There was never another bitch that held a candle to me until December resurfaced! I did cause chaos at the detail shop, and that cost him some major ends! Serves him right!

I didn't know where that bitch lived, but I did know where she worked from her social media profile. I decided to disguise myself and enter the Citizen's Hospital. I would have her paged to the car garage, saying I was a relative or some lie. If I could find her car, I could wait until the end of her shift and follow her home. So, on this particular day, I did just that. I called the information desk and asked for December Cruz. I knew she worked in pediatrics, and I also knew that her and Smoove grew up in an orphanage together. I told the phone attendant that I was an old friend from St. Francis, and I was parked on the second level in the parking complex.

I ducked down in the driver's seat and waited for hours, just to see if the bitch was going to come walking from either exit point. I checked in with my mom, who was hounding me about her timeframe! She needed to sit her old ass down somewhere. That casino wasn't going anywhere! After two o'clock, I felt defeated and crunk up my car. Maybe she was off today. If that was the case, the phone attendant could've said that! I checked my rearview mirror, and to my surprise, I saw the bitch walking casually through the parking lot.

I felt my adrenaline rushing and saw red before me! This was the bitch that was in my way! She was the one that was cuttin' off my time with

Smoove, and I had to eliminate her at all costs. I originally planned to follow her to wherever she was going after work, but I was filled with so much rage, that I put my foot on the gas, ready to run her over. Her back was turned to me, and it appeared as if she was fumbling through her purse for her keys or something. At that instant, I floored the gas and floored it! Her body bounced off the hood of my car, and I didn't stick around to see her body drop. I exited the car garage swiftly, got into the midday traffic, and headed through town as if nothing happened.

I hope I killed that dumb bitch! I smirked at my accomplishment. *Smoove isn't allowed to be happy when I'm over here miserable. I warned him to cancel that bitch!*

***

More than an hour had passed, and I hadn't received a call from Smoove about his fallen bitch. Perhaps he hadn't heard about her accident yet. It really made no difference to me. I called my mom and lied about the crowded mall and the shopping lines. I did have a slight dent in my hood and decided to get it fixed before any speculation came my way.

I pulled into the hood detail shop, Smoove's competition, and blew my horn a few times. The overweight and balding mechanic approached my ride in oil-stained overalls and a crooked smile.

"Hello, pretty lady." He smiled and showed his gaps from missing teeth. "How can I help you today?"

"Yes." I cleared my throat and tried not to pop off because I needed to be nice to get what I wanted from him. "I was shopping at the mall, and when I got to the parking lot, I noticed some damage to the hood of my car! I was so upset. Someone just bumped into me, and I don't wanna ride around with my car looking like this!"

"Hmm, I see." He placed his dirty hand across his chin and examined my car fully. "I can see the dent there. Looks like you hit something; that's for sure. But have no fear, I'm just the man to get it fixed for you!"

"Sounds fantastic." I smiled and flirted a little bit with him. "Just run me the price and we can get this taken care of right now."

"Hold up a second, Miss." He halted my joy. "I didn't say I could get to it right this second! It is the holiday season, and I have a few appointments ahead of you. You could leave the car here with me, and I could get to it sometime tomorrow afternoon."

"It's gonna take that long?" I pouted and whined. "I was really hopin' that we could come to a better understanding. I was really in need of my car; I have a daughter that I must transport, and I can't imagine totin' her around in an Uber or bummin' rides! Is there any way we could get this handled right away? Just name your price."

I seductively dipped forward to show a hint of my cleavage to the horny old man and counted out a few hundred-dollar bills to pique his interest. He stood there, salivating, and I knew I had him right where I wanted him. Regardless of the situation, pussy ran this world, and men were always weak to it!

"You are a beautiful young lady." He nervously wiped the sweat from his brow with a wrinkled handkerchief. "Why don't you step out of the car and follow me into my office in the back? I'm sure we can come to some type of agreement."

I smiled and winked, but I for damn sure wasn't about to sleep with his smelly ass. Maybe he wanted to feel on my titties or some perverted shit like that. I was down for the kink, but I would throw up if I had to sleep with his ass! I exited my vehicle and swayed my hips fiercely while I followed him into his office. He offered me a seat across from his desk, and he sat on the edge of it.

"So, what's your price?" I spoke up because I was becoming anxious while he stared at me like an all-you-can-eat buffet.

"My normal price is $400 because I have to suction out the dent and apply the right coat of paint for the crack in it. But you are looking so delicious to me right now. I might be able to get started on your vehicle right away if you would let me taste you."

"Oh, really?" I plastered on a fake smile but felt the chunks bubble up in my stomach. Just the thought of his ugly ass touching on me was enough for me to knee him in the nuts. But I needed to cover my tracks, so what other choice did I have? "I've never been the type to turn down some head. I just hope you're good at it."

I slowly removed my black, leather tights and my see-through Victoria's Secret thong. The old pervert hastily sniffed my panties and placed them in his back pocket. I guess he wanted a souvenir to remember the moment. I opened my thighs and placed either one over the arms of the chair while I tilted my head back. While he gobbled and slurped on my hidden treasure, I envisioned Smoove between my legs. That man knew how to please me like no other. I felt myself squirt in the pervert's mouth several times, and he also tossed my salad.

"Damn, you're so sweet." He wiped his mouth with my panties. "I could munch on you all day, little lady."

"I'm glad you enjoyed it almost as much as I did." I lied but didn't want to insult the man because I needed his services.

"My dick doesn't work much anymore, but my tongue stays sharp." He chuckled while I laughed on the inside. "Well, a deal is a deal! I will get started on your car. Do you have any plans for the next hour or so? I will just move back my other appointment, so I can get you on your way. I hate to see you go. I hope you come back and see me some time."

"If I'm on your end of town, I will come through and see you." I lied once more because I never planned to return to this dump. "I don't have any immediate plans, so I will just hang out in here while you get to work."

"Alright, sweetie." He licked his coated lips once more. "Help yourself to a soda in the fridge. I also have a few snacks in there if you're hungry."

I nodded and smiled while he exited the office and sighed from that sexual encounter. I checked back with my mother and helped myself to a soda and chips. While I waited on my car, I received a blocked call and immediately answered it.

"Hello." I smiled.

"BITCH! WHAT THE FUCK HAVE YOU DONE?" It was Smoove. I guess he was pickin' his stupid bitch off the pavement where I left her ass.

"Excuse you," I shrieked sarcastically. "Is that any way to respond to someone on a phone? C'mon now!"

"WHERE THA FUCK ARE YOU?"

"With that kind of tone in your voice, why would I tell you that?"

"Willandra, stop playin' with me!" he hissed. "I know you hit December! No one else had any reason to come for her. Just admit the shit and turn yourself in! Don't make me come lookin' for you!"

"I don't know what you're talking about, babes." I remained calm. "I've been at the mall doing my last-minute Christmas shopping! You can ask my mother if you don't believe me. You said somethin' happened to December? Aww, that's too bad."

"Miss me with the fake concern." He cut me off. "You claim to be at the mall, but it's awful quiet in your background, and it's never that quiet in the mall. So, try again, BITCH!"

"I'm not gonna be too many more bitches!" I grew angry and felt disrespected. 'I told you that I have been shopping all day. I'm in the parking lot of the mall. I have to go by my mom's and pick up Angel if you must know!"

"BITCH, I'MA PUNISH YOU ON SIGHT!" A female voice that was unfamiliar screamed through the phone. "YOU KNOW WHAT IT IS!"

"Who tha fuck is this?" I laughed uncontrollably.

"This is Temeka," she replied. "You should know me by now because my fists remember your face! Pull up on me, bitch! Because I'm with all the shit!"

"Girl," I giggled. "I don't give a fuck about what you're with, and I'ma need you to fall tha fuck back because you don't want these problems! Tell Smoove that the next time he calls me, it better be about us. I could care less about his bitch or what happened to her ass!"

I hung up the phone and blocked the number. I didn't have time for their bullshit! I glanced out into the work area and saw the pervert was still working on my car. I alerted my mother that I was finished shopping but needed to run by my house to hide the presents before I picked up my daughter. She seemed okay with the idea, and within the next hour, I was on my way home.

I fired up a piece of a blunt that was in my ashtray and revealed in the misery that I caused my boo. He would learn not to cross me if it was the last thing I taught him. I pulled into my driveway, exited my vehicle, and entered my home. Since I told my mom I needed to put away gifts, I decided to stall for time and take a quick shower. After I lathered my body several times with my Victoria's Secret Love Spell body wash and lotion, I found a cute PINK sweatsuit and placed my hair in a messy bun. I was ready to head to my mother's home when I heard a loud crashing noise from outside of my house.

I peered through the living room window and saw an unfamiliar grey Dodge Challenger in front of my house. The loud banging was coming from my driveway. I grabbed my 45 from my bed stand and approached the front door.

"BRING IT, BITCH!" It was one of those twins that hung out with December, and she was bashing my car with a metal baseball bat! "Oh, you got gun play, huh? Square up, hoe! I know you're the one that got my girl in the hospital! Don't be scared now, bitch!"

"I'ma kill yo ass!" I placed my gun in my purse by the door. Clearly, she wasn't about that gun play, and I didn't mind beating her ass because she was the closest thing to that bitch, December. Maybe I could put her in a hospital bed next to her ass.

"Let's do this!"

We commenced to rumble while my neighbors watched from their yards. I was certain a few of them were recording the whole ordeal. This bitch was really givin' me the business, but I managed to climb on top of her and pound her head in.

"I can't believe y'all started the party without me." I heard another female voice approach me.

"Get off my sister, you bitch!"

I felt a strong tug of my ponytail as I was dragged off the girl and was stomped by both of them. I tried to swing on them but was overpowered by the two of them. My ribs, back, and head were pounding from the beatdown, and suddenly, I heard the police sirens in the background. The two of them continued to beat me until the officers got them off me.

"I want to press full charges on them!" I cried through swollen lips. "These two viciously attacked me at my home that I own! I did not invite them here, and one of them destroyed my car!"

"That bitch got exactly what she deserved!" The most radical twin spat her venom. "She hit my best friend with her car earlier today! She's in the hospital right now! She's the one that needs to be arrested for attempted murder!"

"She also caused our friend to lose her baby!" The other twin revealed.

The officers ended up arresting all three of us after the paramedics examined our cuts and bruises. Smoove had to have given them my address because they weren't smart enough to know that for themselves. Once again, he had crossed me. The twins were released on bond, but I was still in a holding cell because of the hit and run accusations. I had gotten my hood fixed, so I sat there calmly while I waited to be released.

"Willandra Sparks!" I heard a man call my name, and I sat up in the jail cell. It was cold, clammy, and smelled like corn chips. "You have been requested in the interview room. Please walk this way!"

I made my way into the seated area and watched the two detectives emerge into the room. I was ready for whatever bullshit they brought my way. Cops never intimidated me because I was from the streets.

"I'm Detective Hamilton, and this is my partner, Detective Edwards." The Latino officer paused after their introductions. "I can see that you were in a vicious fight with two ladies, Keya and Temeka Cross, today. But the reason we are still holding you is because of the hit and run accusations. Did you, in fact, hit December Cruz with your car in her work parking lot? Please do not evade the truth from us because we will issue a warrant to seize your vehicle and have it examined for her DNA! At this point, you will only hurt yourself by lying to us."

"I want to speak to my attorney!" I fired back at them while I rolled my eyes. I wasn't too worried about them finding anything on my car because I had it fixed. But was it possible for them to find

DNA on my vehicle? I wasn't going to give them a damn inch. They would have to prove that shit! At the end of the day, Smoove should have taken my threats seriously and cancelled that bitch! He was the real reason she got hurt, not me.

-11-

December
Filling My Empty Space

The last thing I remembered was entering the parking lot and heading to my car after my shift. I did have a hard time finding my keys because I felt my phone buzz, and I thought it was D'Angelo calling me. While I looked for my keys, I felt the impact of a car, and my vision went black after that. I found myself hooked up to machines in the very hospital I worked, and I had quite a few unanswered questions. D'Angelo was asleep by my bedside, and he held my hand in his own. I wiggled my fingers slightly and was unable to speak because of the tubing down my throat.

My sudden movements caused my man to awaken, and he smiled heartily at me.

"Baby." He immediately kissed my hand and forehead. "I'm so glad you're awake. I didn't think you would ever wake up. I'm going to go tell our friends and family while I alert the doctor."

SANTA BABY, BRING ME A DOPE BOY FOR CHRISTMAS

I saw him exit my room and wondered how long I had been in here. Had that much time passed? D'Angelo made it seem like I was asleep for quite some time, but I honestly couldn't remember. My body ached, and I felt a few tears trickle down the sides of my face from the pain. After a few moments, Dr. Fletcher and one of my fellow nurses emerged with D'Angelo behind them.

"December." Dr. Fletcher approached my bedside. I had worked with him for the past few years. He was an excellent ER doctor, and I felt safe in his care. "I'm so glad that you are awake. You've been in a coma for the past week and a half! I will remove the tubing from your throat now."

I took a deep breath while he removed the tubing, and my throat felt raw. D'Angelo handed me a cup of water, and I eagerly sipped on it.

"How are you feeling, dear?" Dr. Fletcher continued with his questioning.

"I feel like I was hit by a bus," I whispered with a slight smile on my face. D'Angelo continued to hold my hand, and I noticed the sadness on his face. "I still can't believe I was out of it for so long. It doesn't seem that way to me."

"You sustained significant trauma." Doctor Fletcher looked over my charts. "Two broken ribs, fractured arm, and a concussion as well."

"But what about?" I motioned down to my stomach and saw a few tears drop from D'Angelo's eyes. I already knew the answer from his face, but I needed confirmation. "I mean, I had recently found out that I was pregnant! I'm not sure how far along I am."

"Due to the trauma your body endured from the hit of the car," Doctor Fletcher spoke softly, "I'm so sorry, December. But you did lose the baby."

"NOOOO!" I cried and felt the pain from my injuries immensely. But no physical pain could ever match the hurt of losing my baby. "WHY? WHY DID THIS HAPPEN?"

"I'm so very sorry." Dr Fletcher repeated. "I will leave the two of you alone. I will have one of the nurses come back a little later to check your vitals and administer your meds. You are in my prayers, December!"

I was inconsolable, and D'Angelo tried his best to comfort me. I just cried and cried without the ability to stop those tears. I thought about the vicious way I was conceived into this world. I was so happy that our baby was conceived from love and not a rape like my mother. I had plans to be the best mother I could be. I had the means and the man to be a success. Everything in my life had finally begun to fall into place, and with one swift hit from a car, my life was tragic once again!

"I'm so sorry, babe." D'Angelo cried along with me. It was the very first time I recalled seeing him cry this way. D'Angelo was always the strong one and never allowed me to see him when he felt vulnerable. I now understood why he refused to say goodbye when I left him years ago. The pain was too much for him. At this moment, he showed me all of him, and I fell deeper in love. "I know you was lookin' forward to being a mother. But babe, I'm so blessed to still have you in my life. We can try again, babe. We will try again! It can never replace the child we lost, but you know you got me for life! We will have that family that you always wanted. I promise you that."

"But why, babe?" I sobbed. "What did I ever do to deserve this?"

"You didn't do anything wrong, babe." He rubbed my head and kissed my hand. "This is all on me, babe! I never should have walked away from you years ago! I was afraid to let you see me cry my eyes out, like right now. I was so angry and so hurt that you could ever leave me! But I owed it to you to speak your peace, and we could have stayed in touch. I just didn't know how to share you with anyone, and I just didn't want to let you go! Blame me, babe! I didn't pay close enough attention to Willandra's threats to ending us! But I told her a hundred times that it was over between us. I never strung her along! I may be cutthroat in the streets, but I didn't come at her sideways about us! I didn't protect you; I failed our baby! Put it all on me!"

I watched my man drop his head onto my lap and cry. I rubbed his head and upper back. As much as I wanted to hate him for bringing that bitch into my life, I couldn't do that! It wasn't his fault that she couldn't let go of him. I knew that D'Angelo would never put me in harm's way. That was never a part of our relationship. Had it been in his power, he would have traded places with me in this hospital bed.

"Babe." I soothed him and brought his teary-eyed face towards mine. I gently kissed his lips and tasted the saltiness from his tears. "I won't let you take the blame like that! Yes, she was your ex, but you couldn't control her actions! I know it was hard for you to say goodbye to me years ago, but we have moved past that! The only thing that matters is the fact that love brought us back together! We have a second chance to right all of our wrongs and live our lives together."

"Aww." I heard my ratchet friend, Temeka, in the background. "Y'all are so peachy perfect and shit!"

"Chill out, Meka!" Keya hissed at her twin. "I think it's beautiful that the two of them are so in love. I can't wait to find my soulmate."

"Girl, you so extra." Temeka popped off. "I'm just glad I got my 'Mr. Right Now'! That nigga, Figga, can't get enough of my chocolate drop!"

"TMI, bihh!" Keya rolled her eyes. "But anyways, how are you feeling, sis? You had us all worried, for real! Your aunt left for work not too long ago. I'll have to call and tell her that you are finally awake."

"Yeah, boo." Temeka smiled and kissed me on the forehead. "You really had us shook! We been campin' out at the hospital like we don't see this place enough, sein' how we work here!"

"I love you too, Temeka." I laughed at her. "And thanks for being here, you guys! I can't believe that crazy bitch hit me with her car! Like who does that?"

"A crazy bitch!" Temeka answered the question. "But don't you worry, me and sis got in her ass!"

"What?" I shrieked.

"Hell yeah." Temeka popped her gums. "The day you got hit, Smoove called that bitch and asked her about the hit and run. Of course, her ass denied it. But she was on the phone laughin' like the whole thing was a game! I told that bitch to pull up and come see me!"

"You wanted her to come up here to the hospital while I was unconscious?" I frowned.

"Bihh, pull up just means pull up!" Temeka rolled her eyes. "Anyways, she said some more stupid shit and hung up the phone! You know I was hot like fire, so I told Smoove to run me her address! Keya tried to hold me down in the hospital, but you know she can't overpower me!"

"Girl, stop!" Keya inserted. "Yo ass wasn't goin' anywhere! The only reason you got up was because I had to pee! Don't play yourself like that!"

"Anyways," Temeka threw up her hand to silence her twin, "I rode to tha bitch's house and bashed her little car in! Took my bat with me and tore that funky lil' car tha fuck up! I wanted her to come outside boxin' because I was ready to give her the damn business!"

"I know you lyin'." I shook my head in disbelief.

"You know I don't play about you or Keya!" Temeka made a believer out of me. "I was handlin' her ass too, and then sis showed up! We stomped that bitch for a minute until the cops showed up!"

"Yeah." Keya nodded. "She was talking about pressing charges on us, but we mentioned your hit and run to the cops! We bonded out later that day, but they kept her stupid ass!"

"I just can't believe she took it that far." I frowned and felt on my empty womb.

"Karma is a bitch, boo," Temeka replied. "I hate you lost the baby, and that was one of the main reasons I plowed into her ass! But we still got you here, sis! You and bruh can make more babies. He's down for you! You know if I thought he was with the shit, I'd have to handle his ass!"

"Chill out, lil' gangsta!" D'Angelo chuckled. "Don't worry. I'm on the job!"

"Sobrina, mi Corazon! (Niece, my heart!)" Aunt Camilla walked into my hospital room and showered me with kisses. "Keya messaged me, and

I floored it all the way over here! I'm surprised I didn't get a speeding ticket!"

"I love you too, Auntie." I smiled while she embraced me.

"I'm glad they apprehended that crazy punta (bitch)!" my aunt spat. "They swabbed her car for your DNA and found some. She will be prosecuted in January! I can't wait to see her in court! They better watch out for me; I've always had a mean left hook!"

"I know that's real, TT." Temeka popped off.

"If I get the opportunity, I will sneak her ass in the courtroom!"

"Ain't nobody got time for that." Keya frowned. "Y'all both going to jail for fightin' in the courtroom! Chill out!"

"I appreciate everyone in this room." I felt my eyes tear up once more. "Each one of you mean the world to me and having you all here with me allows me to know that I can face any obstacles head on. I won't let this setback define me! I will mourn the loss of our child, but one day, God will bless us with another one!"

"That's such a beautiful way to view it, mi corazon (my heart)." Aunt Camille smiled.

"God has blessed you with family and a man that genuinely loves you. Nothing could ever top that!"

"I don't know about that one, Auntie," D'Angelo spoke up and cleared his throat. "You were right about all the things December was blessed with, but she could always have more."

D'Angelo knelt on one knee by my hospital bed. There were 'ohhs' and 'awws' from my family, and I just cried from the joy of it all.

"December, you complete me! When I see you smile, my heart smiles! And I know that no matter what obstacles I'm faced with, if I can just see that smile, I know that everything will be alright! When I'm not around you, I'm thinkin' about you nonstop! You are in my prayers every night, and there's no one else that I could imagine spending my life with! I know you been through the whole wedding thing once before, and this is kinda short notice, but I want us to get married on our special date!"

"The number eight?" Temeka blurted out and heard a few hisses from her sister and my aunt. That girl knew how to make the sweetest moment ghetto fabulous.

"The number eight is just a special way that we signified a date for us." D'Angelo shared our secret with them. "It stands for January 1, 2006! It was the day we became official and made love for the first time. We told each other that we would be together forever and always! 1+1+6=8!"

"This is just sweetness overload!" Temeka clapped.

"Sis, if you don't shut tha fuck up right now." Keya scolded her.

"I swear." Aunt Camille agreed. "Go ahead, D'Angelo! We promise to be quiet!"

"Thanks, Auntie." D'Angelo chuckled and brought his focus back to me. In his left hand, he held a velvet-colored ring box. As he opened it, I was in complete awe. It was a 5-karat tear-drop diamond in a platinum band. "Always and forever, babe! Will you marry me?"

"Nothing would make me happier, babe." I cried while he placed the ring on finger. It fit perfectly. "This is the best early Christmas and birthday gift! I love you and can't wait to be your wife."

SANTA BABY, BRING ME A DOPE BOY FOR

CHRISTMAS

My life was not a picture-perfect situation, but I still managed to find love and the life that I was destined to lead. D'Angelo and I had found our way back to one another. No crazy bitch or accident could ever break the bond that we shared together! I looked forward to a full recovery and facing my attacker in court! Santa may have brought me a dope boy, but fate and God brought my better half back into my life forever.